Reshad Fe

Breathe, for God's Sake!

*the Kindness
extended to
me On Cronin Wa?*

*Reshad Feild
(Richard)*

Reshad Feild

Breathe, for God's Sake!

Discourses on the Mystical Art and Science of Breath

Chalice Publishing

First edition

Published 2013 by
Chalice Publishing
P.O. Box 1139, D-46509 Xanten, Germany
www.chalice-publishing.com

Book design by Robert Cathomas

Printed in the US and the UK by Lightning Source
Printed in Germany by Books on Demand GmbH

ISBN 978-3-942914-08-6

Contents

Discourses

Practices

Poems and Quotes

Preface

*The effect of your breath is entirely
your own individual responsibility.*

IF YOU ARE ALIVE, YOU ARE BREATHING. BUT IF YOU
are breathing, you are not necessarily alive. We walk
around in a dream state, in a dream world, identified
with the illusion of cause and effect, and mostly we are in-
capable of doing anything creative except in great
moments. All real inner schools from the beginning of
time have stressed that we are asleep. Jesus certainly said so
often enough. What about his disciples when he asked
them to stay awake while he was going up the mountain to
pray? Jesus told them all to "watch and pray" while he was
away, but when he came back they were all asleep. If you
want to be awake during the time you are meant to stay
awake, be aware of the breath and your breathing.

G.I. Gurdjieff said that we are "cosmic apparatuses for
the transformation of subtle energies". What could this
mean? It surely points to the fact that we should not underestimate ourselves. But we have to be awake and transform our lower nature, or the *nafs,* as they say in the Sufi
language, in order to know ourselves. We are not dogs at a
Kraft's dog show, where little biscuits are waiting at the
other end of our performance, and we shouldn't behave as
such. Rather we need to remember that there is no reward.
If we realize that there is this great world of love within us,
imprisoned by the demanding self, and if we work on ourselves, we may "free the imprisoned god within us," as

9

Kazantzakis said. The god is imprisoned within our illusions, our greed, our negative emotions. In breathing there is a very good start for this freedom to emerge.

The effect of your breath is entirely your own individual responsibility. We create our own atmosphere and the atmosphere around us. The responsibility of knowing this is absolutely enormous. You can walk, let's say, straight into a hospital waiting-room which is full of fear and angst, and if you just try to be in the Divine Presence and breathe consciously, without projecting your own concepts on the outside as to how it should be, this can completely change the atmosphere in that room. If 'you' can do *that,* then *what else* can you do? But if you do it for a selfish reason and think that *you* are going to change the atmosphere, then who is going to try it? It is your ego – and that is not the breath of life.

But what made *you,* dear reader, pick this book? Was it just out of curiosity about yet another interesting subject? Or is it indeed because you have come to marvel at this great enigma of breath and maybe started to wonder what it could actually mean *for you?* I do hope for the latter, because without a genuine question and an honest wish to really dig deep into this mystery of breath, which is inseparable from the mystery of life, you are likely to just keep gliding on the surface of things and to miss this wonderful possibility for real transformation in your life.

Without our unconditional love and gratefulness for life, we will never know the wonderful mystery of breath. We can do all the practices we want, we can even stand on our head and clap our feet – it won't help. Without love and gratefulness, prayer won't work very well either. Why should anything work, if we are not grateful? "All prayer starts with praise," says the Christian tradition. "Gratefulness is the key to will," said Jalaluddin Rumi. And there is only *one absolute will.* Without gratefulness, all our endeavours and struggling will lead to nothing.

This book is aimed at rousing your deeper questions as well as your realization that there is far more to the art and science of breath than might appear on the surface. It does require perseverance and regular practice to come to understand; and there are many, many levels. But all these levels are within you. What this book can do, God willing, is to help you start uncover the latent potential within you. I pray it does, and I hope you will persevere in digging deep. It takes time to come to understand the mystery of breath in all its aspects, and you will have to practise a lot.

The practices you find in this book are completely safe and can be done as often as you feel appropriate. In fact, they seem to be 'so simple' that, over the years, many students have left our esoteric school because they were "bored". But why are people bored? Probably because there is nothing glamorous to achieve. To learn about the Mother's Breath is only a beginning – and it is a beginning without an end.

If people persevere long enough, there may come a time, God willing, when, even while talking to somebody, they are "on top of the breath" and the octave of the Mother's Breath moves through them. Time takes on a completely different meaning. Then, for instance, they know the time to begin with something, and they know when it is complete, when there is nothing further to do or to say. They know what is needed in any given moment, as is so beautifully related in Lev Tolstoy's story *The Three Questions.* When we are on top of the breath, not identified with our emotions and our problems or with this and that, we may *hear* and *see* what is happening. Thus, we can be at the right time and the right place to help others.

∂⋆

Introduction

The first thing in working with breath is humility and gratefulness.

AS "TODAY'S METAPHYSICS IS TOMORROW'S PHYSICS,"

I am sure that before too long many important things will be published on the subject of breath even by established natural scientists. Take, for example, the consequences of the combination of the two facts that the human body consists of eighty-five percent water and that breath contains moisture. This is simple common knowledge. But what if I told you that it directly relates to the esoteric meaning of the expression "to walk on water"?

At the turn of the millennium popular books were published about the crystals in the water, which sold millions of copies. I have been quite outspoken about them because, according to the knowledge I have been given, they can be misleading. Somebody believes what someone else believes and so forth – and there goes the herd instinct. The first book showed how the crystals in the water change with sound. Then the author went further to show that you can take a bottle of water from a pure source and write "love" on the outside, and the crystals in the water will change. Everybody got very excited for a couple of years and ran around carrying bottles of water with "love" on it or the name of a Bach flower or something, and a lot of people made handsome sums of money. Recently, however, two German scientists produced a small book explaining that it is not the *writing* of "love" on the bottle which changes the crystals – it is the precise *moment* that the writing is done and what *attitude* the writer is in.

The readers of my second book, *To Know We're Loved,* will remember that statement at the very end, when my dying friend John on his deathbed said: "Breathe with me, it is time." Interestingly enough, I have never heard a comment on what that sentence means from anyone of the hundred thousands of people who have read that book. What would you say? Do you think, because John was just about to die from haemorrhage, it means: "Breathe with me because it's time for me to die"? You underestimate things a lot if you do! That would be listening literally, listening in a box, and not listening to meaning.

There are many, many levels in this sentence. What about: "Breathe with me, it *is* time"? What is time? Is there time when you are dead? Why do the Sufis say, "Die before you die"? Why is it said in the Koran, "Christ will come before the end of time"? Why is it said in Zen, "If you meet Buddha in the street, kill him"? Because there is no room for two. John was already 'dead' when he was dying. He was complete in himself. Thus, being with him and breathing with him had a very profound effect on me and indeed, even if they did not get to the bottom of it, on thousands of people who read that book – just that one sentence!

Breath is an incredibly vast topic about which hundreds of books have been written. Today, breathing is being discussed in biology, physiology and medicine as well as from psychological and therapeutic perspectives. And yet, do we know *what* breath is? Advice on how to achieve everything from "better health" to "more success" through the latest breathing techniques has been given by all sorts of 'experts' in courses and self-help books. But do we really care about *the meaning* of breath?

Deeper knowledge about the topic can surely be found in religious scripture. Almost all spiritual and mystical traditions know something about breath. Certainly in the Hindu and the Buddhist traditions, such as in Yoga and Vipassana, breath plays an important role. The Abrahamic religions, too, give hints as to the tremendous meaning of breath. And, of course, most native traditions around the world, such as the American Indians, know about the mystery of breath.

I have learned about breath from many different traditions and schools throughout my life. To this day I have never stopped to ask questions, to be amazed and to further study this wonderful subject. I received my first 'breathing lessons' at an age of four in kindergarten. Later in life, I learned from the Tibetan Buddhist tradition, the Druids, Sufism and esoteric Christianity, from the teachings of G.I. Gurdjieff and P.D. Ouspensky and from the Sioux Indians in America.

Over the past forty years, I have been teaching the spiritual meaning and the esoteric aspects of "the mystical art and science of breath", as I call it, to hundreds of students in England, the United States, Canada, Mexico and Europe. I have written about it in many papers and books, and given innumerable talks and lectures on this inexhaustible topic. But "breath" goes on to intrigue people, and they keep asking me how to breathe properly and how to find a right attitude towards life through the breath. This book is a rich compilation of many of my teachings on the subject, complemented with poems and quotes from different traditions and authors, all of which point towards an understanding of breath.

The practical side of what I teach includes some seemingly simple practises which are based on what is called the Mother's Breath. This balanced breathing in a 7-1-7 rhythm holds a great secret that has been hidden in very old documents, going back to the Gnostic gospels in Christianity and earlier. I even discovered it in hieroglyphics of ancient Egypt.

In the art and science of breath we are asked to accept, intelligently, that when we breathe in consciously – by giving loving attention to all the gifts that God gives us and by knowing that He is the only Provider – we get what we need, and this energy will flow to the right places within us. Later on, more specific knowledge, on the electromagnetic fields and how they are related to the *chakras,* the endocrine and the nervous system and so on, may be given. But the first thing in working with breath is humility and gratefulness. It takes humility to accept that mostly we are functioning like machines and are not conscious enough. And it needs gratefulness to acknowledge the fact that we are alive. If only we could understand the sacredness of life and realize it is the only one we have got; that knowledge alone brings us into humility. And humility will bring us into dependence. When we are in total dependence, our breath can be the breath of compassion and we can be true witnesses to the unity.

❧

The Breath Inside the Breath

Kabir Granthvali

Are you looking for Me? I am in the next seat.
My Shoulder is against yours.

You will not find Me in stupas,
not in Indian shrine rooms, nor in synagogues,
nor in cathedrals,
not in masses, nor kirtans,
not in legs winding around your own neck,
nor in eating nothing but vegetables.

When you really look for Me,
you will see Me instantly – you will find Me
in the tiniest house of time.

Kabir says: Student, tell me, what is God?
He is the Breath inside the breath.

Breath Is Life

*Breath is possibly the deepest mystery
of all things in this life.*

THE SECRET OF LIFE IS IN THE BREATH. WE COME
into this world on the breath and we go out on the breath,
but if we are not awake to breath we will surely die asleep
to the reality of life itself. Breath is life. Without it there is
no life. But we presume breath, just as we presume life. It
happens, and we just go on living unconsciously, until
finally we are presented with death and wonder what happened to life. Unless we are conscious in breath, we are
asleep to life. The average man, living his life in a mechanical way, forgets all about breathing until the moment of his
death, when he struggles to draw the last breath, clutching
to the remnants of what he has known as life. It is so easy
to take breath for granted, but it is really an obligation in
our lives to learn how to breathe consciously. If we are
living life passionately and really love being here, we will
want to explore the depths of this great miracle.

The spiritual world is right here, in life. It *is* life. And we
cannot be here, we cannot even be alive, without breath.
Few people can accept the responsibility of being alive,
which is to inhabit this body and be custodians of this
planet. This requires tremendous respect. We are not just
our bodies, our emotions or our thoughts, but we must
totally inhabit the vehicles we have been given, through
which we can express the spirit of life. That is what it is all
about. And the secret to this is in the breath. In many

languages "spirit" and "breath" come from the same root word. The spirit of life is carried on the breath. To be conscious of life, we must be awake to the breath. In fact, it is not even *possible* to be conscious, in the true sense of that word, without being awake to the breath.

Can you make love consciously without being awake to the breath? Can you prepare food consciously, being awake to the life within the food, without being aware of the breath? Everything is within the breath or, as it was put in the thirteenth century by Muhyiddin Ibn Arabi, one of the great Sufi mystics, "All is contained in the Divine Breath like the day in the morning's dawn." You can breathe in any colour you want, any element or vibration, from anywhere in the world, without leaving the room. It is all possible. It is not difficult and just takes practice. Healing is carried through the breath, telepathy is carried through the breath, and the transmission of *baraka,* spiritual grace, is carried through the breath. Think of the wind. It blows and carries with it whatever is light enough to be lifted from the earth. It carries the scent of flowers. It carries the leaves as they fall from the trees. It carries the seeds from the plants to where they may take root.

The possibilities lying within the understanding of breath are enormous, and the greatest challenge is to be continually awake to it. Can we learn to breathe with life? Can we learn to breathe with God? To breathe with God we need to surrender to God or, as Jalaluddin Rumi said, "If you want to live, die in love; die in love if you want to remain alive." This is the passion of surrender that we need in order to reach union with God. It is surrender, not achievement. There is nothing for you to achieve. There is only *one* Absolute Being unfolding from the essence of

Itself into every single moment and through every single being, and it all happens through the breath.

The awareness of breath is necessary every day, every moment. We can begin by watching the rise and fall of the breath. This itself takes much practice, and few people are prepared to make the necessary effort. When we can just watch the breath, we will start to realize that we are continuously being tyrannised by thoughts that move us this way and that. Although we do not like to face the truth, it may become clear to us that we have little permanence. What we think 'we' are is constantly changing. We might realize that we are not our thoughts, any more than we are our emotions or our bodies. Why do we find it so difficult to watch the breath without being moved all over the place by thoughts? Until we learn to breathe consciously and develop a permanent 'I', or 'observer', we can always be led astray. Only when we learn to breathe in awareness can there be a chance to come upon the inner being that is our real self.

Unless we are on top of the breath, in awareness, we cannot hear; we cannot even begin to know of our inner being because we are still involved with our lower nature and the chattering of the mind. Unless we are on top of the breath, we cannot begin to be of service because we are not really here in the present moment. When we are on top of the breath we have the possibility to give something to the world and the future to come. We are here to give, to give all of ourselves, in total commitment to life. This is what we are asked to do in return for the gift of life that has been given to us. It is useless to talk about 'self-development' or even 'self-fulfilment' if we cannot breathe out consciously with love and compassion.

Without conscious breath there can be no flow of life energy. The energy of life is all around us, and we can consciously bring it into us for our use and then give it back in service. A teacher of mine once gave me the instruction, "Breathe in only to breathe out." Eventually there ceased to be any sense that I was breathing; I was being breathed. This can only happen when the in-breath and the out-breath are balanced, which means that we are in harmony with the Divine Flow of life. In harmony we have the possibility to help one another.

Breath is possibly the deepest mystery of all things in this life. Everything is contained within the breath. All life is available to us through breath. As we breathe in, we can breathe anything we need, from any place in the universe. And as we breathe out, we can give something of ourselves back to life, helping create a pattern for the world to come. Our breath is not limited by walls. We can breathe in from all directions, consciously breathing in what God gives us, and breathe out to anywhere it is needed. We can even choose the quality of our breath, and that quality depends upon our degree of awareness. Remember that there is one thing we all share, and that is air. We are potentially a cosmic apparatus for the transformation of subtle energies, but without the breath there can be no transformation. There can be no purification of life without the breath.

People do not realize that something is being born out of every moment, and that if we could find the right rhythm of breath that is most natural and most in harmony with the universal laws governing our existence, we would have the possibility of contributing to the work of bringing about peace on this planet. Through the breath we can be of service to life by coming into harmony with it.

There is a breath of the womb of the moment. It is the breath of the matrix of life. Like the physical womb of the mother, it contains the matrix of possibility for life on earth. The present moment 'pulsates', expanding and contracting, coming into existence and passing out of it instantaneously. Everything is born from this rhythmic pulsation of the womb of the moment. This rhythm also produces the waves of vibration that make up the subtle or formative worlds interpenetrating this physical world of form. All of these worlds interpenetrate each other, each with different rates of vibration. Everything depends upon the rate of vibration, just as sound creates pattern and pattern creates form. We can tune into the higher rates of vibration through the refined quality of our breath. There is infinite possibility lying in the 'here and now'. Within this breath, which I call the Mother's Breath, is the whole octave of life. With every act of love we make, with every conscious breath we take, a child is being born – maybe not a physical child but a real child nonetheless. This is a great responsibility, that we can bring forth something new into the world through our love and through our breath, in every moment of our lives.

The Moment

Muhyiddin Ibn Arabi

The moment lengthens and shortens in accordance
with the presence of the one who partakes in it.
There are those whose moment is an hour or a day
or a week or a month or a year or once in a lifetime.
And [included] in humanity is the one who has
no moment.
For the one who is heedful of the breaths
has the hours in his power, and all that is beyond that;
and the one whose moment is the presence of the hours
loses the breaths;
and the one whose moment is the days loses the hours;
and the one whose moment is the weeks loses the days;
and the one whose moment is the years loses the months;
and the one whose moment is his lifetime loses the years;
and whoever has no moment has no lifetime
and loses his afterlife.

The Universal Rhythm

*When you are in the present moment, you are awake
to the rhythm of the octave at all times.*

A BEING IS BORN TO THIS WORLD HAVING AS ITS
basic rhythm the breath of the mother at the time of conception. If you breathe beautifully there is a rhythm, and this rhythm is in harmony with your own nature as well as with nature itself. I am referring to the rhythm of life, into which we may more or less consciously fit. Because it is such an extraordinary way to come into harmony, the practice of 7-1-7 breathing has gone into many fields, such as hospitals or midwifery, where it is of tremendous value.

Nobody expects you to understand the importance of the 7-1-7 breathing in just a few days. Sometimes people have difficulties with it because they are trying too hard. The fact is that the rhythm which is going on in the universe is 7-1-7-1-7 all the time anyway, and the 7-1-7 breathing is to do with the natural pulsation of the womb of the moment. The teaching of the 7-1-7 breathing, or the law of the octave, goes back to 2700 BC at least and has been handed down in a partly hidden knowledge. You can see it, for instance, in the hieroglyphics in the Egyptian pyramids. Be that as it may, it is a cosmic law and an incredibly beautiful one once you understand it. But there is a riddle here. If you try to understand it, you will think – and then you won't understand. Therefore the answer is: just do it!

The first thing to learn is that it doesn't matter how slowly or fast you breathe. It is to establish this natural rhythm which is the octave of life. Everything is moving along this beautiful waveband of *Do-Re-Mi-Fa-Sol-La-Ti, Do-Re-Mi...* etc. Just breathe in to the count of seven, and in the pause you don't stop – it is rather like a leaning into the next wave on the ocean. Or, for those of you who are dancers, it is like that incredible feeling in the 'pause' when you are just about to go from one movement into another. It really is much more difficult to talk about than to experience it. You breathe in to the count of seven, pause one count, breathe out to the count of seven, pause one count, and so forth. It is all one continuous movement.

I remember one of my students who so very much wanted to understand this. Unless one *wants* to understand, there is no reason why one should. She decided to take her summer vacation and walk across France on a continuous 7-1-7 breathing. At the end of it she knew what it meant. When I was learning all this in my early twenties, we just literally would do nothing but breathe in and breathe out and count. When the counting became natural, we didn't have to count any longer; it was just there.

When you are in the present moment, you are awake to the rhythm of the octave at all times. It is as though you stand in the ocean and the waves keep going along. This is the real meaning of "being on top of time". You can either *observe* it or *be* in it, and you can even choose whichever situation you want. You won't be subjected to the tyranny of time anymore. But it does require practice and loving attention. Eventually it becomes like a dance, very beautiful. And it will be perfectly possible for you to continue talking, or doing whatever you do, and still be in the 7-1-7 breathing. To some people, however, it remains a mystery.

❦

All Is Contained In the Divine Breath

MUHYIDDIN IBN ARABI

All is contained in the Divine Breath
Like the day in the morning's dawn.
The knowledge transmitted by demonstration
   is like the dawn for he who drowses;
So that he sees that which I have said, as a dream,
   a symbol of the Divine Breath,
Which, after the shadows, consoles him of all distress.
He has long ago revealed Himself to him who came
   to fetch a fire-brand,
And who saw Him as a fire, whereas He is a Light
   in the spiritual kings and in the travellers,
If thou understandeth my words, thou knowest
   that thou hast need of the apparent form:
If Moses had searched for something other
   than the fire,
He would have seen Him in that, and not inversely.

❦

The Mother's Breath

A Practice

THE BREATHING PRACTICE THAT I TEACH IS FOUNDED
on a natural rhythm which is sometimes called the Mother's
Breath. This is the rhythm of 7-1-7-1-7. It is based on one
of the great cosmic laws of the universe, the law of octaves.
Much was written about this law in P.D. Ouspensky's
book *In Search of the Miraculous.*

The practice entails breathing in to a count of seven,
pausing for one count, and then breathing out to the count
of seven and pausing for one count. The rhythm is the
most important thing and not the precise amount of time
it takes to unfold in each individual. Each person is
unique, and we should find the pace that is most comfortable for us.

For a while the rhythm may be difficult. If our breath is
not in harmony with the pulse of the universe, it will take
practice in order to come back to what is our true heritage.
The womb of the moment *pulsates* at a certain rhythm, and
this is understood through the practice of 7-1-7 breathing.

We have mostly presumed the breath. Although there
are further dimensions to this practice, the first step is to
watch the breath, in gratefulness to be alive in each
moment. We follow the breath as it comes in through the
nostrils and back out again, getting used to the rhythm of
7-1-7-1-7.

Now we can start work with the placing of the breath.
Within us there is something which is sometimes called

"the cauldron", which can be likened to the cauldron used in alchemy, in which the base metals are transformed and turned into gold. In this practice we centre the cauldron in the solar plexus, and we breathe into this area.

When we breathe in, we breathe in not only consciously but, in a sense, selfishly. By this I mean we breathe in what we *need* for the necessary transformation to take place. We can breathe in earth energy, magnetic energy, colour, vibrations from the mineral kingdom, the vegetable kingdom and so on. It is perfectly possible to breathe in from all directions at once, into this central point of the solar plexus. This should be a joyous experience, awakening wonder in the glory of being alive.

The next step has to do with the out-breath. We breathe in only to breathe out. What we have taken in on the in-breath needs to be given to the waiting world on the out-breath. And here, for the out-breath, we move our attention from the solar plexus to the centre of the chest. At the same time we visualize our breath radiating out from that centre in all directions, manifesting as light. Each individual can add their own concepts of love and goodwill towards all of God's Creatures, from the planet to mankind itself. I often give the analogy of the heart centre being like a lighthouse for all the shipwrecked seekers in the world.

Once again, the method of this practice is to breathe in for the count of seven all that we need in the transformation process. On the pause of one count we raise our attention from the solar plexus to the heart centre, and then we *radiate* out in the form of light to the count of seven, before pausing for one count. Then we repeat this cycle over again.

Little by little this practice becomes perfectly 'normal' and we find ourselves in the right place and in the right time, able to be more of service every day of our lives. The road of the Sufi path is also called "the Way of Love, Compassion and Service". When this practice has been mastered, we can feel a sense of true glorification in the privilege of what I call "breathing alive". At last we can truly know that we are loved, since God is love and "there is no God but God."

It is my most earnest wish that those of you who have come upon this message will do your best to make good use of the practice. I am sure that, as the years unfold, you will be given more details to add to this basic rhythm of the universe, the Mother's Breath, the pulsation of the womb of the moment.

2₹

Observe Your Life

AVICENNA

Observe your life between two breaths.
Breath is a wind, both coming and going.
On this wind you have built your life –
But how will a castle rest on a cloud?

2₹

Purpose

*The real purpose of undertaking any breathing practice
is to come to know, little by little, of our true nature.*

IN ORDER TO PROCEED IN ANY SPIRITUAL PRACTICE,
it is necessary to question our personal motive and intention as well as the purpose that underlies such practices. Whether in breathing practices or in prayer, we should want to give ourselves and the rest of the world the best possible opportunity to be of service. And for this we need correct motive and intention. Sitting down for a breathing practice just to have a comfortable half an hour is useless.

We need to ask ourselves whether we are undertaking such an endeavor merely in order to benefit ourselves, or whether we have looked carefully into the nature and purpose of our activities and the responsibility that is necessary on our part if we undertake to learn one particular practice or another. It is so easy to slip into the habit of acquiring yet another breathing practice or whatever. If we are not ready or able to complete what such a practice requires, then it might be preferable if we do not start the project in the first place. Is this not true?

The basis of the teachings I give, as I have stated again and again, begins and ends with what I call "the art and science of breath". I write this because I beg you to really question whether or not you know that you are alive at any one moment – like *right now* for instance. And do you think it is actually possible to know this just by thinking about it? After all, when we stop breathing, we are no longer alive in this world. And yet, it is here in this world that we live in order to learn and finally know who we are and what is the purpose of life on earth.

With this understanding, we can say that the real purpose of undertaking any breathing practice is to come to know, little by little, of our true nature. Although the practices themselves may essentially be very simple, they are necessary. Just as a farmer has to plough his land and then prepare it carefully before he can plant what he will eventually harvest, so we also need to work on ourselves in order to be able to 'come into being' and receive the real knowledge that is so vitally essential in the process of conscious evolution, rather than mere organic evolution. Organic evolution is necessary too, but for real change to come about within ourselves and in our world, conscious evolution is essential – and it is possible.

Unfortunately, it is relatively easy to understand "purpose" with the intellectual centre and with 'intelligent' thinking, but this is *not* enough. If the true purpose that underlies this teaching is to have any genuine meaning at all, we have to deeply *care* about wanting real change in our lives and in the world around us, rather than just the appearance of change. We have to care very, very much. And to do so, we have to love very, very much.

It is only when we are dissatisfied with our life so far, when we no longer complacently seek agreement to our self-righteousness, that we can start to turn around and realize that it simply cannot be enough for us to merely walk around on two legs, disguised as human beings, but yet still unable to control our own feelings and emotions, still missing a permanent 'centre' or a permanent 'I' within ourselves. True, we have been able to function relatively well so far, maybe we even have had good jobs and careers and families and raised our children and so forth – but *do we know who we are?* This is the big question.

Most often it is the very pain that we carry in our baggage that brings us to the point of turning, once and for all, to our true home. When we turn, we no longer need this baggage. And it is the art and science of breath that is one of the most powerful tools which can help us consciously transform the contents of the baggage into something useful without losing the container.

Usually, I advise people who pick up my books or come to my lectures or attend my school never to underestimate themselves. The reason I mention this is because if it is truly destiny which brought us together, then there is surely something within each one of them which both seeks and, at the same time, already 'knows'. "What you are looking for is what is looking." If that which knows finds the right path, the road of truth, the separation is melted away little by little. "Light upon light. God guides those whom He pleases."

※

Your True Destiny

JALALUDDIN RUMI

When you find yourself with the Beloved,
embracing for one breath,
in that moment you will find
your true destiny.

Cross, Triangle and Circle

A Practice

EVERYBODY WHO IS WORKING WITH INNER PRACTICES, such as meditation for instance, knows how difficult it sometimes can be to just sit down quietly and follow the breath. And still, if people want to persevere, it is indeed necessary that they spend a little time each day in actually practising the breath. And that means to try not to lose your awareness even for the duration of *one single* breath.

This was the first instruction I was given in that Buddhist centre where I studied breath in my early years. I had to do nothing but breathe for six hours a day! Of course my mind was wandering all over the place and strange devils came up. But I trusted the teacher, Trungpa Rinpoche, who was one of the most famous Tibetan Buddhists at the time. Because of this trust I could persevere.

To help you with this concentration on the breath, let me give you one little practice. This is an 'old trick' which does not come from our particular school. But it is a very useful trick, and it is not dangerous. I would never give a practice which is dangerous. Again it is not very easy, but it can help. Try to do it for fifteen minutes, if you can, without losing your attention for the duration of a single breath. In order to do it, you need to prepare three cards or sheets of paper with a black pen. On the first card you draw an equilateral cross, on the second an equilateral triangle and on the third a circle.

Now sit about six feet in front of the card and try, while you are watching your breathing, to concentrate on the cross for five minutes. It will start to waver, going up and down and do funny things. Don't worry, continue. If "a dog comes in and bites your leg, do not bite it back," continue. If the cross comes out and tickles your nose, do not try to brush it away like a wasp, continue. The cross represents one aspect of us which we might call "the emotional body". Keeping your concentration on that cross will help you to balance your emotional body.

Next, you turn the second card up with the equilateral triangle. This represents the mental body. Again, breathe and concentrate for five minutes. You will find that one day the card with the triangle is an absolute misery, and another day the cross may be a real challenge. Whatever, keep practising. By giving your best – you cannot do more than give your best – and continuing to breathe, preferably even smiling at the same time, this practice will help you to become able to do the 7-1-7 breathing with much greater ease and, finally, even to break through into that wonderful space of silence where you don't need any support and where you are being breathed.

Lastly, for five minutes do the same with the symbol of the circle, which is more difficult. When you concentrate on it, you have to be in a place within you where you are not staring at it. Somehow you are looking at the circle *and* the circle is looking at you. There is no separation. You will find that the atmosphere will change completely, it is much stronger.

This little practice is useful, but do not become obsessed with it. With Trungpa Rinpoche we had to do it every day, without missing one, for eight months in a row. That was in that particular school, and so I am not suggesting you have to do it eight months in a row. But it is a practice which you can always use, if you find it difficult to sit down and breathe and meditate.

❦

Experience Begins with Breath

Vijnana Bhairava

The One Who is intimate to all beings said:

Beloved, your questions require the answers that come
Through direct living experience.

The way of experience begins with breath
Such as the breath you are breathing now.
Awakening into luminous reality
May dawn in the momentary throb
Between any two breaths.

The breath flows in and just as it turns
To flow out, there is a flash of pure joy –
Life is renewed. Awaken into that.

As the breath is released and flows out,
There is a pulse as it turns to flow in.
In that turn, you are empty.
Enter that emptiness as the source of all life.

Breathing In – Breathing Out

If the breath is limited, life is limited.

PATIENCE IS SURELY ONE OF THE NAMES OF GOD.
For me, it has been one of the most difficult lessons to learn. All of us in the West suffer from the dreaded disease of expectation, which stems from an educational background geared to give us this disease. We have examinations to pass, grades to be numbered and counted, and a sense that there is a reward just around the corner for all of our hard work. Everyone knows perfectly well that money does not necessarily bring happiness, inner peace and contentment, and yet our whole system is based on the acquisition of it. Today societies can topple on the drop of the stock market. What a ridiculous situation! How then can we readjust our thinking in order to understand the path of transformation and our direct responsibility for it? It is a good question.

We breathe in only to breathe out. It is relatively easy to remember how to breathe in. We all love to breathe in the aroma of sweet perfumes or the smell of the ocean. We can breathe in the passion of the moment. We can visualize a colour and irradiate ourselves with it. We can breathe in strength and courage. We can sense the gentleness of a flower on the in-breath.

And there is also another aspect of the in-breath. If we are not awake, we may breathe in the results of our own negative emotions or thoughts and even share in those of others. We breathe in thoughts held in the moisture of the breath.

Let me explain it this way. We have seen that when we enter a room, we are all breathing the same air. If you could measure the air in the room before and after a business meeting, for example, it would be different indeed. Certainly the atmosphere would have changed and the atmosphere comes from the moisture contained in the breath. The atmosphere in a church, a mosque or a temple normally has beautiful vibrations. People go to these places to pray, to ask, in humility, for what is needed. They praise God on the out-breath with their singing and chanting. They are not frightened to breathe out, filling their world with love and light. In an atmosphere that is filled with greed, there is endless talking and negotiating, but very little giving. Thus there is imbalance. It is so important to remember the out-breath. We are given so much in life, and it is on the breath that we can give away to our friends and to the very planet itself.

If you open your arms, first to the side, and then bring them up above your head, the hands touching, and finally bring them forward in an arc, the fingers touching and the arms extended in front of the centre of the chest, you have defined your own universe. In other words, your universe is within the extent of your arm-span. Imagine your hands as being the extension of your heart centre so that you could stretch out and breathe through your hands as well as your nostrils. You could touch a beautiful leaf or a flower and, in recognition of its beauty, breathe in. Then you could breathe out the essence of the beauty that you have breathed in, thus filling up your universe with love and light. You truly have something to give.

The trouble is that we find, if we are truly honest, that the vibrations on the out-breath do not travel very far, rarely as far as the extent of our own arm-span. It is as though we have been so stifled and repressed in our lives, that the pain is somehow trapped. Yet, if we breathe in beauty, pain can be transformed and then the out-breath is pure, moving out into a waiting world.

What happens between the in-breath and the out-breath? The reality of the moment stands right in the middle of those two breaths, and it is only when they are truly balanced that we can know what lies hidden there. If the two breaths are not balanced, that which wants so desperately to be released remains imprisoned within our hearts. That is why the teaching of conscious breathing is so important. We can fill up our heads with conceptual thinking, but the prison doors remain locked.

The first time I came upon this idea I was living in a Zen Buddhist monastery in Japan. I was young and perhaps that was why the importance of the balance of the two breaths did not mean enough to me so that I would really work to perfect the breath. Many years later I went on a retreat to another monastery, this time run by Tibetan Buddhists. I went with every expectation in the world, deciding I was definitely going to find an answer to my questions. We were told, when we arrived, that if we wanted an interview with the Lama, we must sign our name on a waiting list. We would then have twenty minutes of his valuable time. I signed up immediately, and a few days later I was told when I could see him.

I remember going into the Lama's room in a state that could be described as a mixture of expectation and sheer terror. He was sitting on a cushion and indicated that I was to sit opposite him. He spoke very little English, which did not make life any easier. I tried to explain my problems.

He just looked and smiled, nodding frequently. I don't think he really understood a word, but it didn't seem to matter. Towards the end of the allotted twenty minutes he said, "Very good. You breathe in only to breathe out. You start today, six hours please." The interview was over.

I went back to my little room, trying to get used to the idea. I had come a long way and all I was told was that it was necessary to sit down and breathe for six solid hours every day. No further explanation was offered. I didn't even know what a lotus sitting position was, and of course there were no chairs in the meditation hall.

There were about twenty-five people staying in the centre and, at that time, several visiting Lamas, who started chanting soon after 4.00 a.m., when we were all meant to get up and begin our meditations. I hadn't the slightest idea what they were chanting. There were a lot of bells and gongs which were struck at appropriate moments. It was all very mysterious, but after a few days I settled into the rhythm and things quietened down considerably.

Those six hours of breathing were still worrying me! Luckily I had been provided with a hard, round cushion to sit on and I knew that I was meant to keep my back as straight as possible. I plucked up courage and went down to the meditation hall. It was dark, lit only by candles. The air was thick with the smell of incense. In the gloom I could see about ten other people sitting and, presumably, breathing. It was very difficult not to feel self-conscious in such a situation.

I felt hopelessly naive, but closing my eyes, I began. Breathe in! Breathe out! I cannot remember just how long I sat there that first day. I reckoned that it was all right to divide the six hours into sections. Anyway, my legs went to sleep, my back hurt and nothing happened at all. I do not know what I expected, but whatever it was surely did not materialize. There were no bright lights, no flashes of understanding. There was, however, a lot of rumbling in the stomach area, I remember, because the food was not to my taste at all.

I got through the first day and steeled myself to start all over again the next. Luckily there was one man I could talk to and we went for a walk that evening. He was equally English but had been working at this practice for some years. He was very courteous and patient with me and told me to persevere.

To cut a long story short, I persevered breathing in and breathing out for six hours a day for a whole week and then I asked to see the Lama again. This time there was a translator, which helped matters considerably. I tried to explain, as politely as possible, that I had breathed, that I found it impossibly difficult to remain awake, that thoughts kept crowding in from all sides and that so far nothing had happened! "Ah-ha," said the Lama. "Very good. Now eight hours a day, please." The translator smiled, the Lama smiled and I tried to smile. Now it was to be eight hours of sitting in that same meditation hall, with a lot of silent people all around me and that dreaded incense. Again I went back to my room to try to recover.

I will say that the next week was very different. Expectation had gone out of the window. In its place came utter and complete boredom! It is true that the breathing was becoming easier and the balance was better, but fitting eight hours into the day was a hard task indeed. The following week the Lama increased the time once more and that was when something started changing. I found myself as though hallucinating. It seemed that every fear and guilt I had ever had started to emerge. The fears manifested in physical pictures. I could swear there were snakes and tigers in the room. I was in a jungle. Finally I was so terrified I asked to see the Lama urgently. This time he looked even happier, smiling and nodding vehemently, when I explained the story to him. He then laughed out loud saying, "Very good, very good! Continue!"

I did continue. Little by little the fears went and there was a dancing sensation in the breath. All the thought pictures disappeared as they were redeemed through the present moment, and I was beginning to get a taste of what it could mean to be "on top of the breath". Time took on a totally different meaning. There were even moments when a flash of real understanding would come. When I saw the Lama in the passageway, he would bow and smile. I did not go to see him again. I knew for certain he had been right all along.

꽃

We Worship the Holy Breath

THE ESSENE GOSPEL OF PEACE

The third communion is with the angel of air,
who spreads the perfume
of sweet-smelling fields,
of spring grass after rain,
of the opening buds
of the Rose of Sharon.

We worship the holy breath,
which is placed higher
than all the other things created.

For, lo, the eternal and sovereign luminous space,
where rule the unnumbered stars,
is the air we breathe in
and the air we breathe out.

And in the moment betwixt the breathing in
and the breathing out
are hidden all the mysteries of the infinite garden.

Angel of air,
holy messenger of the earthly mother,
enter deep within me,
as the swallow plummets from the sky,
that I may know the secrets of the wind
and the music of the stars.

ॐ

Standing-Position Breathing

A Practice

THE PURPOSE OF THIS PRACTICE IS TO INCREASE THE
flow of life force as well as improve your power of concentration. It can also help to open the blocked channels in the etheric or subtle bodies. For this practice, you will need a thick piece of white card about a foot square, in the

middle of which you have drawn a black disc about the size of a penny. The disc needs to be sharply defined, so it is best to use ink or paint. The card is placed at eye level on a wall about six feet in front of where you are standing. The entire practice consists of only twelve breath cycles, and it is preferably done before the meals.

In your hands you will be holding a portion of broom handle, approximately eight inches long and between one to one and a half inch in diameter, one piece in each hand. When the practice has been completed, wrap the pieces of wood carefully in a cloth, and put them in a safe place. Over a period of time, they will gain a great deal of magnetic energy and so should not be treated lightly.

Before commencing, do a few stretches to get the body moving and then take up your position six feet in front of the disc. The arms should be by your sides, the body in an alert but relaxed position with the back straight.

The legs should be slightly apart. If you find that there is more energy passing through the right nostril, then the right foot should be slightly forward. If there is more energy in the left nostril, then it is the left foot that should be slightly ahead of the other. If the breath is perfectly balanced, then the legs should be parallel with the feet slightly apart.

Facing the disc on the white card and remembering the rhythm of 7-1-7-1-7, breathe into the solar plexus on the count of seven. At the same time, slowly rise up on the balls of your feet and clench the wood in your hands with increasing strength – the maximum clenching on count seven – and hold this position for another count. The rest of your body, if possible even the arms above the elbow, should be quite relaxed.

After the seven counts and the pause slowly start to relax your hands and wrists and return to the original position. At the same time, breathe out light in all directions from the centre of your chest area.

As instructed, this practice should only be done for twelve breath cycles and preferably before meals. To complete the practice, do a few more stretches, and then continue with whatever you were doing.

⁂

Asking for His Breath

ZUNI INDIANS

I beseech the Breath of the Divine One,
His Breath giving life and old age,
His Breath of waters, seeds and riches,
His Breath of fecundity, power and strong spirit,
His Breath of all good fortune whatsoever.

I ask for His Breath,
and, into my warm body drawing His Breath,
I add to your breath, now.

Let no one despise the breath of his fathers,
but into your bodies draw their breath,
so that yonder to where the road of our Sun Father
    continues
your roads may reach,

so that, clasping hands and holding one another fast,
you may finish your roads.

To this end,
I add to your breath, now.

ò€

How It All Started

"You breathe in only to breathe out."

I WOULD LIKE TO SHARE WITH YOU THE PERSONAL
story of how I first heard about the 7-1-7 breathing
rhythm, and then how I met up with various people in my
life, all of whom had found this particular path in one way
or another.

With me it all started when I was a small boy. It was
during World War II, and we children had to walk to the
house where the kindergarten school was being held every
morning. Rain, snow, sunshine, it didn't matter; we trot-
ted off down the lane to the big house, where we lined up
in our very short trousers, our hands behind our backs and
desperately trying to keep our eyes facing forward, because,
at the same time, there were frequent battles above us in
the sky between the German and English fighter planes.
We were not allowed to look up or observe anything. We
had to stand there, our eyes facing forward, and wait for
necessary instructions.

The teacher for these exercises was called a "remedial
mistress"! Today, I believe, you would call her a "P.E.

(physical exercise) teacher". I remember so well staring from my very small size at her perfectly white gym shoes, and then following my gaze up her legs, which were covered in thick brown stockings that reached only to her knees. She was immensely tall, and with her chin stuck forward, as it always was, it was very hard to see her eyes. Anyway, to cut a long story short, first we had to do various physical exercises, and then, standing very still, we were told to breathe into the solar plexus area for the count of seven, pause for one second, and breathe out from the centre of the chest, pause, and repeat the practice for up to fifteen minutes. Meanwhile the fighter planes were roaring overhead, and I was doing my best to stop giggling every time I looked at her white shoes.

I still remain eternally grateful for those lessons in kindergarten, even at such a young age. The next step for me was when I studied with Chögyam Trungpa, the famous Tibetan Rinpoche who started the first really large Tibetan centre in the West. It exists to this day and is called Samyé Ling. When I went for my first interview with him, I was expecting all sorts of magical steps to enlightenment. Instead, all he said to me was, "You breathe in only to breathe out." I was then sent away to the meditation room to practice this exercise for many hours a day. The strange thing was that, somehow or other, the memory of those very early days with the remedial mistress came back to me.

Of course, on a far deeper lever, I am sure that from reading these stories you will start looking closer at the positive sides of the memory.

After many more years of travelling, I met with a pupil of Professor Ilse Middendorf. She was a very old lady at that time, and I was – in the words of Jesus, "By their fruits ye know them" – very touched by meeting this woman. After much discussion, I discovered that Professor Middendorf had started her own training in the breath when she was eleven years old, and that she had been in contact with a group of people known by the name of Mazdaznan.

I suppose there is no such thing as chance, because a little later on, when I was living in Los Angeles in 1973, I, too, met with the Mazdaznan. This happened through an Italian homeopathic doctor, who promptly sent me off to the south of France, to what was then a very famous centre, run by Mikhael Aivanhov. At that time, he was the official master of the Great White Brotherhood, which was based in the nearby town of Frejus (although there were other centres in South America). Anyway, I was an invited guest and I lived in a cottage next to *Le Maître*. At the first meal, to my total surprise, with several hundred people present and with *Le Maître* sitting on a stage at the other end of the dining room, we were all asked to sit up, backs straight, in what I would call an actively receptive state, and for fifteen minutes – what did we do? Breathe to the rhythm of 7-1-7-1-7!

You see, if our motive and intention are good, we are given all we need to fulfil the task of being conscious human beings in this lifetime, the only life we have.

꒰

Another Breathing Has Arrived

Jalaluddin Rumi

The Prophet said, "In these days the Breathings
   of God prevail:
Keep ear and mind attentive to these spiritual influences,
   catch up such-like breathings."
The Divine Breathing came, beheld you, and departed:
   it gave life to whom it would, and departed.
Another breathing has arrived. Be thou heedful,
   that thou mayst not miss this one too, o comrade.

⁊ᚴ

Rhythm, Quality and Placing

*"All is contained in the Divine Breath
like the day in the morning's dawn."*

THERE WAS A SMALL GROUP OF PEOPLE LIVING IN

a community in New England who built a 34-foot aeolian
harp and placed it on top of a mountain. As you probably
know, the original aeolian harp, tuned in a special manner,
was made to be played by the wind. These young people
made this unusual experiment together and made a record-
ing of the extraordinarily beautiful music of the wind
blowing through the harp. The recordings, made in spring,

47

summer, autumn and winter, had a profound effect on me when I first heard them.

The first step towards a deep understanding of breath is to learn how to breathe in a way that our subtle bodies are finely tuned in the same way that the harp was tuned to respond to the wind. It is so easy to take breathing for granted and forget that it is an obligation in our lives to learn how to breathe consciously. However, if we live life passionately and really love being here, we will come to want to explore the depths of this great miracle called "breath".

When the wind changes, we know that something different will happen in our world. There is the wind of change blowing over the face of the earth even now. Where and how does the wind start? Scientists can tell us many technical things about this, but there are other, more profound explanations that can be discovered from inner work.

We too can be played by the wind, and what we speak will be the sound of the moment, bringing with the word the possibility of real change rather than the appearance of change. We all know this somewhere deep within ourselves, and although God gives us everything, it is up to us to be so finely tuned that the music that is played is of truth itself. Did not Jalaluddin Rumi say, "We are the flute, but the music is Thine"?

Breath is the secret of life, for without breath there is nothing. With correct breathing it is possible to choose the way you wish to travel. Think of the wind – it blows and carries with it whatever is light enough to be lifted from the earth. It carries the scent of flowers, it carries the leaves as they fall from the trees, and it carries the seeds from the plants to the place where they may take root. There is a great message here! We come into this world on the breath and we go out of this world on the breath. The average man, living his life in a mechanical way, forgets all about breathing until the moment of his death when he struggles to draw air into his lungs, clutching to the last remnants of what he has known as life in this world.

The practice of breath can be done every day, every moment, for the rest of your life. It seems easy, but as each moment is different, at times you may find it impossible to concentrate. But little by little you will come to understand the importance of what I am telling you.

First, you must learn how to purify the subtle bodies by surrendering the concept of the physical body so that you may come upon that invisible matrix from which the body is continuously being formed. If you learn how to purify yourself, you will be able to see more clearly as the thought forms and projections that obstruct clear sight and inner hearing begin to dissolve. After all, thought is the only thing that divides us.

Make sure that your back is straight, and then simply watch the rise and fall of the breath. To be able to do this takes much practice, and few people are prepared to make the necessary effort. When you can just watch the breath, you will begin to realize that we are tyrannized by thoughts that move us this way and that, almost constantly; and although we do not like to face the truth, it becomes clear to us that we have little of permanence. But you are not your thoughts, any more than you are your emotions or your body. If you are not your thoughts, and yet you find it so difficult to just watch the breath and not be moved by these thoughts, then is there not something wrong?

Until you have a permanent 'I' you will always be in danger of being led astray. When you learn to breathe in awareness, there is a chance to come upon this inner being that is your real self.

There are three major aspects of breath. The science of breathing is the study of a lifetime, but these three aspects, if considered carefully and put into practice, can help change the course of your life. They are the rhythm of the breath, the quality of the breath, and the positioning of the breath.

Much has been written recently in the West about the rhythm of the breath, called *pranayama* in India, but people do not realize that the different kinds of rhythms taught by different schools and teachers are meant to produce different results. If you want to drive a car very fast up a hill, the engine takes on quite a different rhythm than when it is coasting gently down the hill. The speed of the car may be the same, but the rhythm of the engine is quite different. It is the same in the science of breath – the understanding of rhythm is vital.

The rhythm I am teaching you is sometimes called the Mother's Breath. People do not realize that something is being 'born' out of every moment, and that if we could find the rhythm that is most natural and most in harmony with the universal laws governing our existence, we would be contributing to the work of bringing about peace on this planet.

Make sure your spine is straight, so that the vital fluids can pass easily up and down. Now, inhale to a count of seven, pause for one, and breathe out for a count of seven. Before breathing in to start the second cycle, pause once more on the out breath for a count of one. This is a very simple rhythmic count of 7-1-7-1-7. If you work hard, the timing will soon become automatic.

Let go of all concepts. Surrender to the rhythm that flows and pulsates throughout all life. This rhythm is called the Law of Seven, and by following it you establish yourself as part of the harmonious principle of life, which wishes only to conceive perfection from within itself. The Mother's Breath helps us to see the infinite possibility lying in the here and now, like the physical womb.

This rhythm of the breathing helps us to see that the present moment pulsates, expanding and contracting, coming into existence and passing out of it again instantaneously. Everything is born from this rhythmic pulsation of "the womb of the moment". This rhythm also produces the waves of vibration that make up the subtle or formative worlds interpenetrating the grosser physical substance. It is all just a question of different rates of vibration. The slower the rate, the denser the material; the higher the rate of vibration, the more refined and less stable the substance. And the rate of pulsation is the same as the rhythm of the breath: 7-1-7-1-7.

The next stage is concerned with the quality of the air you breathe. Just as the wind carries on its wings whatever is light enough to be lifted from the earth, there are many qualities that can be carried on the breath if we understand rhythm, and if we are able to concentrate correctly. For example, you could choose one colour out of the whole spectrum and breathe it into your body, infusing each cell. This practice is useful in certain types of healing. You can breathe in a strong vibration, similar to the low notes of the piano, or you can choose to breathe in the finest vibration imaginable which, in this world, would be beyond the range of sound. You can choose anything! You could breathe in the elements of fire, earth, air or water. You could breathe in the essence of a particular flower or herb. The science of breath is a vast subject, known only to a few in the past, but now it is time for the world to begin to understand.

The third aspect I wish to touch on is the placing of breath. Just as the wind carries the seed from one place to another, so the breath can carry intention from one area of the body to another for special purposes. Through correct placing of the breath we can learn to bring the body into balance. We can begin to learn the art of transmutation, the art of the alchemists. We can begin to fulfil our responsibility in being conscious human beings devoted to a life of service on earth.

❧

A Hole In A Flute

HAFIZ

I am a hole in a flute
That the Christ's breath moves through –
Listen to this music.

I am the concert
From the mouth of every creature
Singing with the myriad chords.

❧

Once Upon A Time

A new breath was born.

ONCE UPON A TIME, WHEN THE WORLD WAS VERY young, there was harmony. There was one rhythm, one breath, the breath of unity. The world turned. Once upon a time. But once upon that time, that one moment, a new rhythm evolved from the rhythm of harmony. A new breath was born. There came another sort of time upon the time of natural order. From the Breath and Rhythm of God there came the breath of man… Once upon a time.

So there came about two rhythms, two breaths, and the tension created by the two brought about the two great Commandments: "Love the Lord, thy God," and "Love thy neighbour as thyself." Then there could be harmony once again.

But mankind has never remembered, and so at certain times of history we are offered, once again, the chance to turn straight to our Lord, to take the path of return. We are offered the chance when things seem to be at their worst, when order has failed and chaos rules, when mankind has forgotten to love, when God has been forgotten.

۶

The Scent of the Archangel

Suleyman Dede

If you are a seeker,
Fall down upon the ground in prostration.
That you may see
What kind of mood there is
In His pure Grace.
There they will give you incense
And in its fragrance
You will smell the scent of the archangel
And the Secrets of the Giver.

🪰

Breathing for Another Person

*Only if you have permission, trust, love,
humility and gratefulness.*

SOMETIMES I AM ASKED, "CAN ONE BREATHE FOR
somebody else who is in need of help?" It is the same thing
as with praying for other people. The answer is: yes you
can. But in breathing, as in praying, for another person
permission is vital. Readers of my generation in England
and in the United States may remember a method called
"mind control", a wave that became quite popular in the
late 1960s and early 70s. According to that approach, you

can alter somebody's whole attitude. I am not judging the man who invented this method, but when I read about it I knew that something was wrong. I discovered that people in these groups were praying for other people, and they were doing so without their permission.

The power of prayer is tremendous if you know how to pray. Even if you don't, the consequences can be enormous. Look at the suicide bombers, these tragic figures of young men who have all been led astray by the abuse of the holy Koran, from which they have been instructed to repeat certain passages over and over until they are horribly brain-washed. If they internalize solely one aspect, it can easily turn into fanaticism; and before they know what has happened, it becomes their *reality.* Do you think, for example, that praying or breathing for people who try to control others, in this case who try to turn young kids into suicide bombers, will help or do any good? On the contrary, it can only make things worse, much worse.

For many years, I had a quite successful healing practice in England. Eventually, when I met my teacher, who himself knew a lot about healing, he told me to give it up because he saw that I was much too attracted to it. One of the things I learned from him was that with cancer, for instance, you must never put your hands on the area of the cancer itself because you only make it worse. Cancer is a 'chaotization' of cells. You need to heal it from a much higher level. If you treat something in the uterus of a woman, to give another example, you don't treat it through the uterus, you treat it through the throat centre, which is the second harmonic of the second *chakra.*

Similarly, if you pray, don't pray *for* things. Turn to God. "Thy Will be done, not mine." That's how I start and finish every prayer. Don't think *you* are going to help. Remember, you are meant to be 'non-existent'. Turn to God, and *then* you may be of help. But to pray – or to breathe – for somebody who's *reality* it is, say, to exterminate Western culture as we know it, would only increase chaos.

Sometimes it is not possible to get direct permission from the person in need of help; in this case you must ask permission of God. I teach my students how this is done; you must ask an inner question. You have to ask *from* your heart *into* your heart. The Hesichasts in Eastern Christianity used to do it by dropping their head on their chest and trying to hear the answer. In our school, we seek permission before making any important decision by asking: May I? Should I? Can I? These three questions – remember that three is the first number – can save your life, which is God's Life on earth. But when you ask, you've got to be absolutely in trust. "May I?" is asking permission of the Highest, "Should I?" is common sense, and "Can I?" is to do with one's own state. *If* you get three yeses, you have to do it – even if you don't want to! On many occasions when I got three yeses, I had to do things which I didn't find logical and I landed up in trouble – apparently. Yet in the end, it always did somebody some good.

When I was studying esoteric healing, I had many wonderful teachers. One was an incredible, most extraordinary woman. After she died, which was just lately, there was a whole page on her in *The Guardian.* One of the things she taught us was how to get people out of a coma. You can't always succeed with this, but sometimes it works. This does not only refer to physical comas, by the way. There are all sorts of comas. Gurdjieff said that we are "sleepwalkers"; that is also a kind of coma.

How often are *you* in a coma? Imagine a 'tone scale' with death at the bottom, followed by coma as the next higher state, and then further up comes grief in its various forms and then there are ten further steps in that scale. The method we were taught to get a person out of a coma was the following. You become a mirror for the person who is lying, let's say, in a hospital bed. In respect and love ("seek the level of those with whom you speak, so as not to humble or distress them") you go to a level which is just slightly higher than where that person is – and you breathe. If that person twitches a finger, you twitch the same finger just a little bit more. But not too much, or else the person will go back inside. This way, little by little, you may be allowed to help somebody out of their coma. But you have to *breathe* for them (if you have permission). Why? Because they cannot be conscious enough to breathe for themselves.

It is also possible to be on the breath with somebody who is dying. Sometimes this can be very, very valuable. Edith Wallace, a good friend of mine and a pupil of John G. Bennett, had a Jewish friend whom I never met. He lived in New York and, like Edith, was a Jungian psychologist. About thirty years ago, he had picked up my book *Breathing Alive* and later learned that Edith knew me. One day when he was in his nineties, Edith called me in Santa Fe and said: "My friend in New York is dying within two or three weeks. Could you please speak to him?" So I rang him up and he asked me, "Can you teach me?" Having read my book, he obviously thought I must know something. In the background, I could hear the wailing and the Hebrew prayers going on in his apartment. I told him to first send out the rabbis and his family in order that we could talk. Then I said, "Now breathe with me in this rhythm of 7-1-7-1-7, into the solar plexus and out of the heart centre. I will breathe with you." So he did, and we breathed together for some time. And indeed I could 'hear' – I am not referring to voice or sound – that something was happening. He was incredibly grateful. After about one week, he was on his death bed. He called me, and again we breathed together until, finally, he died consciously.

Yes, you can breathe for another person. If you have permission and if you have enough trust, love, humility and gratefulness, you can. If you are awake to what others need, not what you merely think they need, God may bring you what is needed.

෧ඦ

With Every Breath Return

Sun Bu Er

If you want the elixir to form quickly,
First get rid of illusory states.
Attentively guard the spiritual medicine;
With every breath return to the beginning of the creative.
The energy returns, coursing through the three islands;
The spirit, forgetting, unites with the ultimate.
Coming this way and going this way,
No place is not truly so.

෧ඦ

Being of Service Day In, Day Out

If we are on top of the breath,
we live in the ever present moment and that is
the only time we can be truly of service.

MANY BOOKS HAVE BEEN WRITTEN ON THE SUBJECT
of breath, particularly in the Yoga tradition, but remarkably little material can be found in the Western world, for the Western mentality. In considering breath, I first want to stress the word "service". There is so much pain and suffering in the world. Often within ourselves it is hard to sit down and complete a practice, such as a breathing practice, as an act of serving the world, when perhaps we are in great pain ourselves. The paradox is that often when we do remember that we are here to serve, things ease up for us in our own lives and we are offered a flash of what our purpose may be.

Most of the time we are asleep and we presume many things, not the least of which is breath itself. Breath is life! If we contemplate these three words alone, we can understand our responsibility in being conscious of our breath and also gain encouragement in learning how to breathe under all circumstances. In our contemplation we can say *breath* is life, breath *is* life, or breath is *life,* each emphasizing a different aspect of breath to be discovered. In order to be truly awake, we need to understand the importance of breath. We can, for example, follow the breath through the nostrils and watch its circulation in the body. We can see its transforming effect on the cells and molecules, and know that it can be a carrying force of healing energy to those parts of the body that need it.

Our breath is not just limited to our own body, but can be transmitted across time and space. We can also learn how to breathe for another person when the going gets rough. Breath is the key to conscious birth, sex and death. Consider the man who stands by his wife through labour and at the moment of birth, keeping the strength and rhythm of his breath constant, so that it is easier for her to relax. Conscious breathing is also vital in the sexual act, which can be the most sacred act on earth if we wish to consciously participate in the Divine Order. And, at the moment of death, even if the person who is going to pass is unconscious, by breathing consciously, using the Mother's Breath, there can be deep peace in the room.

Obviously, all this needs a certain degree of practice. Unfortunately, few of us were taught such things at school or in our homes, but it is never too late to learn! The great key towards learning the art of breathing is not to expect, however subtly, any reward from the practice. The mind is ambitious, but we must remember that we are here to serve and be transformed, not to gain power and favours for ourselves.

Let us look at a typical day, beginning with the moment we wake up, and observe the implications of breath. Perhaps we yawn or stretch a little until we are ready to get out of bed and begin our day. When we are lying horizontally, our breath is not the same as when we are sitting or standing. Both positions bring in different aspects of energy. When we are lying down, we have a certain type of magnetism, essentially related to the time of day when the sun sets and we begin our night-time journey towards sleep. Equally, when we rise from bed into a vertical position, we have an energy of a different order, necessary to complete our work during the day. In the same way, if we breathe consciously while lying on our right side, we find a different sensation to breathing while facing the left. That is why it is said that if we are unable to pray standing, sitting or on our knees, then we should pray lying on our right side. The quality of the breath is more receptive in this position.

If we are absolutely awake and conscious as we get out of bed, we are able to blend-in breath, the word and the sound of the different aspects of night and day. The first practice in the morning is to decide to get out of bed, as opposed to just haphazardly rolling out and drifting aimlessly into the day. We consciously get up, being awake to the exact moment that our feet touch the ground. The bed will surely wait for us for another night! Sitting on the edge of the bed, we then offer ourselves to the beginning of the new day, saying within, "May I be allowed to be of service this day." At this time we also say the prayer of our choice before we stand up, and then, remembering the breath, we move into the next step of our lives. It is amazing how helpful this is.

The morning proceeds. We eat breakfast and then go to work. If we watch carefully as we move through the day, our breath starts to change. It is as though we have a built-in gearshift in the tides of our breathing which alters according to what is apparently going on in the moment.

Let us say, for example, that we get into our car, drive towards our place of work and suddenly find ourselves in a traffic jam. Imagine that we left a little late from home, which increased the rhythm of our breath, and now, from the fear of being late, we start to develop anger and frustration because things are not going the way we had hoped they would. The breath, accelerating from our fear of being late, gets stifled in anger. In both these states, we could not be true agents for true service. In the first instance we would not be in the present moment through speeding along in hope, and in the latter case we would also not be in the present moment through the stifling of our breath. If we then lost our temper and shouted at the other drivers, we certainly would not be of service and we might even cause an accident. True transformation can only occur in the present moment.

The same applies to our emotional lives. If we are on top of the breath, then our consciousness is not submerged by our emotions. However, most of us get it backwards. What consciousness we have is totally immersed in a sea of emotional turmoil.

But there is hope! Through learning, first of all, why it is useful to breathe, and then learning how to breathe, we can once again get on top of the breath. The higher aspects of our being, interconnected as they are with the higher worlds themselves, can then work through us, carried on the wind of change that blows through a conscious man or woman. This is the necessary change from stagnation, illness and negative emotions. It is a great challenge.

We all make mistakes, otherwise we would never learn. Let us say, for the sake of this analogy, that we continue to forget about breath and service during the day. We arrive late at the office and storm through the door. We find that there is a new secretary, and the letters that we were meant to write are misplaced. The coffee is cold; and then, just as we are making a fresh brew, the power goes off. At this point, about the only thing that could save the disastrous day would be the remembrance of the sacredness of breath. If we worked with the Mother's Breath, the office would calm down and order would prevail once again.

Breath – conscious breathing – has a direct relationship to time. Our experience of time completely alters if we are on top of the breath. If we had left home at the time we decided we would, having said goodbye to our husband, wife, children or friends for the day, stopped for a moment to collect ourselves, smiled as we got into the car, and *decided* to drive consciously to the office, then perhaps there would have been no traffic jam. If we had left on time, we might have gone straight through all the other drivers who had not made their own decisions and therefore were still caught in the traffic jam!

The day continues at the office. Just as each hour is different and has its own feeling, so does each day. What we do on a Monday, which is influenced by the moon, we would not do on a Tuesday, influenced by Mars, or on a Thursday, influenced by Jupiter. Each day has its own quality. In the same way that planting at certain cycles of the moon increases the chances of the plants being healthy and strong, so, by planning our activities in conjunction with the particular quality of each hour during the day, we can establish order and balance in our own lives.

If we watch the breath during the day, we will find that approximately every hour there is a subtle change, not just in the rhythm but also in the positioning of the breath. These changes happen automatically although we seldom notice them at the time. Usually, there is more 'vibration' or energy going through one nostril than the other. If we are aware of our breathing, we may, at one moment, be able to sense the breath more easily through the right nostril and then again, at another moment, through the left. When we feel more energy going through the right nostril, we are in a position of being more positive and it is a good time to take action. Equally, when the sensation of breath is in the left nostril, we will be more receptive. If the breath is equal on both sides, we have a balance between the active and the passive.

We can change our breathing from one nostril to the other as the need arises. If it is necessary to attend a meeting in a positive manner, then, in the space of about three minutes, we can change our breath to pass through the right nostril. If we are ready to receive what we need to hear in anyone moment, then it is important to have the correct vibratory rate going through the left nostril. It is much more difficult to get into the totally balanced breath; but with visualization and practice we can learn to breathe through the membrane that separates the right and left nostrils.

The more we work with conscious breathing, the more we will be able to live in harmony in a chaotic world. We will find that we identify less and less with situations and thus can stand above the grinding clash of opposites in the bank or supermarket. Gradually we begin to build in an inner observer that is more sensitive to the moment, and so we are able to see what is needed at anyone time and also to know how we can best help.

If we are sitting in a room with a group of people, we are all apparently breathing in the same air and breathing out the distilled air after it has passed through our systems. Yet there is also a way of choosing the air we breathe, although only by making the experiment ourselves can this be shown to be true. It is well worth the trouble taken. The key is to choose the finest *quality* of air that we can. This is done with what is sometimes called "creative imagination". It is not fantasy, but rather an inner gift which can be brought forth as a creative act.

A question might arise as to how we can choose the finest quality of air in a room full of smokers. The answer is that it is difficult but still possible through visualization. By judging the smokers or the smoke, we become identified with the situation. If it is vitally necessary for us to attend a particular function, the presence or absence of smoke should not be our sole deterrent. Our aim, remember, is to be able to breathe under all conditions.

We can imagine that we are standing by an ocean or by a beautiful stream or pure mountain water and, holding this picture, continue to breathe with the Mother's Breath, the 7-1-7-1-7 rhythm. It is also possible to breathe from a particular star or planet for balance. If we need extra male strength, we can breathe from Mars, which will increase the element of iron in our bodies. If we need to be more receptive, we can alternatively breathe while visualising the planet Venus, increasing the element of copper within us. We can even visualize, as we breathe, the sacred places on the planet, which are of so much benefit to the world. We might imagine the places in the Himalayas where the holy men assemble, or cities like Jerusalem, Chartres in France, Glastonbury in England or the huge medicine wheel in Wyoming. It is all done with breath and visualization, and the gift is ours.

Let us return to our imaginary day. If we eat consciously during the lunch break, respectfully watching the breath, we will have all the energy that is needed for the afternoon.

Our attitude towards food should be the same as that in breath. It is important that we do not take anything for granted in our lives and that we remember to be grateful. We can then share this deep sense of gratitude with others who might have forgotten it.

The afternoon can be a sleepy and difficult time to concentrate. Once again, if we use the breath consciously, we can make things much easier. Each breath may be our last. We never know. We come into this world on the breath and we go out of this world on the breath. If life seems difficult, during the afternoon or at any other time, we can always sit down for a moment and contemplate this.

Soon it will be time to leave the office, get back into the car and face the journey home and the fumes, the frustrated human beings, the blaring radios and the toll gates. It all seems to take so much time. How do we manage to deal with such situations day after day without getting an ulcer or high blood pressure? Many people put themselves into a totally numbed state, which is one solution, but it is not a conscious way. It is merely a method of being totally unconscious, so that the discomfort need not be faced.

If we are on top of the breath, we live in the ever present moment and that is the only time we can be truly of service. As I have said, we all have to serve our own way. We must be conscious and awake. We need to be present at every breath we take. Freedom lies at the exact point between the in-breath and the out-breath, and at that moment grace may enter. We never know when this might happen. It could happen on the motorway. The traffic jam may be an excellent time to practise the art of breathing, so that by the time we arrive home, we will be completely ready to greet our friends or family. We will not be carrying all the weight of the day on our shoulders and bringing it into the house. Instead we will be free to be of service from the moment we cross the threshold.

Once we are home, we will probably want to take a bath or shower to wash away the dirt of the day. Here is another opportunity to use the breath. As we bathe, we can consciously breathe in the moisture. Breath carries moisture. Water, on the other hand, is a conductor of electricity, and thought forms are electrical impulses. By being conscious of the breath and the moisture in the shower, we can purify our subtle bodies, where thought forms of the subtlest nature may have attached themselves to us without our noticing them.

Now we are ready for the evening and all that it may bring. We have worked hard to keep on top of the breath and on top of time. For the completion of the day, we make our Decision Practice and finally do the End-of-Day Clearing Practice.* We can then sleep at peace, ready for what the next day will bring.

Breath is life! We breathe in only to breathe out, and thus we learn to balance the in-breath with the out-breath. We watch the breath and see how it enters us, and how it can be used for good. We visualize as we breathe. We breathe for others in times of stress. Through visualization and breath, we gather the beauty and energy we need in order to be of service. As Muhyiddin Ibn Arabi, the great Sufi mystic, once said, "All is contained in the Divine Breath like the day in the morning's dawn."

---

* See: Reshad Feild: *The Inner Work,* Volume I, Chalice Verlag, Zurich 2004.

Man Is Like the Wind

Frithjof Schuon

The nature which surrounds us – sun, moon, stars, day and night, the seasons, the waters, mountains, forests and flowers – is a kind of primordial revelation. Now these three things – nature, light and breath – are profoundly linked with one another. Breathing should be linked to the remembrance of God. We should breathe with reverence – with the heart [...]

The remembrance of God (*dhikr*) is like breathing deeply in the solitude of high mountains: here the morning air, filled with the purity of the eternal snows, dilates the breast. It becomes space, and heaven enters our hearts.

❦

The Tyranny of Thought

The object of all breathing practices is to enable you to go beyond thought forms. Move on.

WHEN I WAS TAUGHT ABOUT BREATHING BY A TIBETAN

Lama, I had to start off with six hours a day breathing in and breathing out – nothing else. No support of music, no comfortable chair or anything. I was to develop the patience, the guts and perseverance to break through that barrier of thought and emotions. Bawa Muhaiyaddeen, whom I am quoting below, said: "Do we take the section of hell" – which we have created for ourselves – "and try to destroy hell? No. We should push it aside and move on." Remember what I wrote about so often in my books: recognition – redemption – resurrection. "There is no need to destroy it. Just move on." If, in your breathing practice, thoughts arise, they can be awful, they can be attractive, but they are all useless. Don't fight them. Breathe and move on.

> If a dog comes to bite us, we just move on. We do not stop and try to bite the dog in return. Similarly, when evil follows us, we should tell it to go away and move on.

Can you imagine how empty the therapists' waiting rooms would become?

> We should not spend time with it. It will shout for a while and then leave. Like this, the world will come swirling at us for a while, but if we do not look back, it will go away. Sins will also follow us for a while, but if we don't turn back, they will go away. They will say, "This is not the place for us," and go away.

So what is this teaching us? Look inside and find out what it is that attracts things. I am not against therapy, as long as it is a very good therapy. But I believe that therapy which concentrates on actually *following* the misery often continues to repeat the problem round in circles, only in different ways.

Many things will follow us for a while. If we look back and smile broadly at them and become happy because of them, then they will overcome us. But if we do not look at them, they will go away, saying, "This won't work. This man will trample me. I cannot enter him."

Sometimes I used to wonder in my old Tibetan days: Why did they all smile so much? It is because they see *through* things.

When you 'come into being', as we say, there is *nothing*. You are no longer subjected to the tyranny of thought. The object of all breathing practices is to enable you to go beyond the tyranny of thought and thus the cycles – particularly those which affect human beings – which are projected and precipitated by thought forms.

Think of the expression, "I am thought being holy thought," which comes from some of the innermost teachings. And Rumi says in the *Mathnawi:* "All begins with thought." So you might also say: "I am thought being holy thought. God protect me from this ignorance." Thought is invaluable. You can't value it, it is too important. The only thing that can be valued in connection with thought is the result of bad thinking, like social gossip, which is the most destructive force on earth.

Don't forget: a thought form has only one objective, and that is to manifest itself. And the only creature it can manifest itself through is the human being. An animal is subject to instincts and feelings. We, because of our greed, ignorance and bad motives, are continuously being besieged by thoughts. And mostly we consider them to be our *own* thoughts. But most of the time they have nothing to do with us; because *who* are we to have these thoughts?

What is the possibility of freedom and of coming into being if we are always being thought?

If we are humble regarding these things, we know how few opportunities we have to really be free of being besieged by thought. The patterns, which repeat themselves in different ways, sometimes even causing psychosis, are composed out of thoughts frozen in time. So, every time you feel haunted by thought, try to say, "Mind your own business!", keep breathing and move on.

ॐ

Don't Get Lost In Your Thoughts

JALALUDDIN RUMI

Don't think, don't get lost in your thoughts.
Your thoughts are veils on the face of the moon.
That moon is your heart.
Those thoughts cover your heart.
So let them go.
Just let them fall into the water.

ॐ

Clearing the Day

A Practice

WHEN WE GO TO SLEEP WE SHOULD BE AWARE THAT there is always something carried through into the next day. If we go to bed and we breathe quietly in gratefulness, a certain quality is carried through into the next day; and a different quality is carried through if we fall asleep with resentment, anger or frustration.

If we can rest grateful for all that has been given to us, whatever it is, there is the sound of gratefulness that echoes in our heart and makes a good atmosphere for the next day. So when we get out of bed in the morning, we walk into a 'cleared space', a space which we have helped create.

Once we know that we have nobody in the world to blame but ourselves, maybe we won't even blame ourselves. Much too frequently, we forget that we all are human, that none of us is perfect.

Whenever we have forgotten, in the evening when it is quiet, we 'turn in repentance'. Repentance is not guilt; it is something quite different. We breathe quietly and in gratefulness until we can feel the "please", the "thank You" and the "I am sorry" all at the same time in one breath. "Please let me remember. Thank You for allowing me to remember that I have forgotten. I am sorry I forgot."

Once we can feel all of this in one breath, then the day is clear for us. The past that had been forgotten is turned through the present moment and goes to make good food for the next day.

Prayer to the Holy Spirit

SAINT AUGUSTINE OF HIPPO

Breathe in me, o Holy Spirit, that my thoughts
   may all be holy.
Act in me, o Holy Spirit, that my work, too,
   may be holy.
Draw my heart, o Holy Spirit, that I love but
   what is holy.
Strengthen me, o Holy Spirit, to defend all
   that is holy.
Guard me, then, o Holy Spirit, that I always
   may be holy.
Amen.

❧

Atmosphere

*Once we remember that we are all sharing
the same air, this brings us towards the realization
of what "compassion" could mean.*

MOST PEOPLE DO NOT UNDERSTAND THAT ATMOS-
phere is created by breath and that, as such, it can be
changed through conscious breathing. In conjunction with
the geometry of the building, the atmosphere in a room is
created essentially by the people in it, and an atmosphere
can remain in a room for a long time.

A human being consists of eighty-five percent water. Breath contains moisture, which is an electrical conductor, and this moisture carries the subtle energy of thought forms, which are electrical impulses. Therefore beware of thinking. Once you come to understand that atmosphere is created by breath, you can start to see that you are, as G. I. Gurdjieff put it, "a cosmic apparatus for the transformation of subtle energies" and how, through the knowledge that is given to us, you can actively and consciously transform atmosphere.

Neither the in-breath nor the out-breath are limited by walls, such as stone or brick walls. Breath is only limited by the walls we ourselves put up, the walls which divide us, such as the walls of resentment, envy and pride. We put them up, and that limits the breath. If our eighty-five percent of water are filled with anger, jealousy, greed, vanity, fear and all these things, then what we breathe out creates an atmosphere which is not necessarily very happy. If somebody comes into a house in a strong mood – weak or angry or something – it can literally eat up the air.

If, on the other hand, somewhere you find a nice atmosphere, it is because of the breath – its ratio and proportion and the love it carries – of you and the people in that place. The patterns of resentment, envy, pride and so forth have been dissolved in love so that what comes out through you on the out-breath, hopefully, comes in the form of light, pure light, which is the "light behind the sun", the light which has no opposite in darkness.

When we love life, we know that even thought is given to us, as all creation comes from a world beyond time as we know it. When we are conscious, we begin to understand that, through our breath, we must create the space for the creative principle of life. It is up to us; after all we are responsible for our planet.

And so the word "responsibility" comes in here. It is only *we* who can be responsible for our own breath, our own life. We may be taught various ways of breathing, even specialized techniques of breathing for special purposes, but only *we* can *do* it.

There is always an echo of His Love in any one breath we consciously take in gratefulness. It is like a bell of recognition. Do not try to walk around manifesting presence. If you are conscious on the breath, you *will* manifest the presence.

Once we remember that we are all sharing the same air, this brings us towards the realization of what "compassion" could mean. Whenever you go on a bus or a train or walk down a street and you pass a beggar by the side, maybe curled up in a ball, and you stop to put a coin into his hat, be aware that both of you share the same air. He may not know it, but with your awakened compassion, maybe something more happens the moment you put your coin in.

So what about actually facing your responsibility for the person next to you? Always when in a group, remind yourself that you are all breathing the same air. Can you take the responsibility for the fact that the person next to you is breathing your air and you are breathing his or hers?

When, as a product of continuous inner work on many levels, you little by little start to realize that you have to be one hundred percent responsible for your own feelings and emotions, it is incredible how you can transform the atmosphere through your breath. And as breath is not limited by walls, the effect of one man or one woman standing proud in the breath, in conviction of life, can be tremendous. There can be an effect on the immediate surroundings as well as on the far greater environment – because there is no distance!

And therefore it is not an illusion to even say that the whole earth can be transformed through a single conscious human being. In the Bible it says, "Wheresoe'er ye stand, there is holy ground." But it doesn't become holy as long as we are asleep. What is a holy man? A human being in who's absolute consciousness the Divine Spirit, or the grace or whatever you want to call it, can manifest wherever and whenever it is needed.

⅗

Your Heart's Sincerity

JALAUDDIN RUMI

The water and clay, when it fed on the breath of Jesus,
    spread wings and pinions, became a bird, and flew.
Your glorification of God is an exhalation from the water
    and clay of your body: it became a bird of paradise
    through the breathing into it of your heart's sincerity.

⅗

The Second Birth

We can be born consciously, we can
make love consciously and we can die consciously.
All these three are dependent upon one thing:
breath.

WE CAN HELP IN THE OVERALL PLAN OF GOD BY
learning to breathe consciously every moment of our lives.
Once we learn to control the breath, we may find the
rhythm of the mother, the creative feminine, from whom
we came and through whom we return to the Source of all
life. When we have knowledge of the love between the
mother and the father of all creation, conscious suffering
becomes an act of joy.

It is easy to talk about "living consciously", but the question remains: can we totally commit ourselves to a life of
service? Until that commitment is made, we can only talk
about what may lie beyond. We have to make the first step,
and then the other steps are given to the extent that we
have the courage to face each moment and are completely
honest. Honesty is the prerequisite of anyone wishing to
understand the nature of the way of love.

The understanding of breath is very important here. We
come into this life on the breath and we go out of this life
on the breath.

Consider the birth of a child. During the period in the
womb, the breath of the child is the breath of the mother.
Only when the umbilical cord is cut does the child breathe

on its own. Imagine the shock that this transition entails. Consider the intention behind that individual breath given at the moment when the child is separated from its mother. Can we see in our own lives our separation from the womb of life and from the breath of the mother herself?

Two types of breath exist in every moment: the natural breath of the Divine Mother and the breath that we, in our illusion of separation, impose on life. When we find the Mother's Breath, that natural rhythm that underlies every moment, we have the possibility of returning to the womb of the Divine Mother, from which we can be reborn. This is called "the second birth". In that knowledge, we are eternally present and eternally being reborn with each breath we take.

When a woman gives birth naturally, it is necessary that she learn how to breathe. The birth of a child is certainly painful in the physical sense. But, if the mother is totally conscious in the breath, she does not identify with the pain. The child that is born, even at the moment of the cutting of the umbilical cord, knows deep within its soul that indeed there is no separation.

If we are the parents of a new age, it is equally necessary we learn the science of breath. This is our challenge and our responsibility: to give birth to the child that we call "the new age", realizing, first of all, that through the knowledge of breath we give the child the chance that has not been granted before. Secondly, we realize that through a completely unselfish attitude of conscious suffering, we may bring this child to fulfilment. There can be no going back. The result of all this is something the mind cannot understand.

Reason is powerless in the expression of love.
Love alone is capable of revealing the truth of love
     and being a lover.
The way of our prophets is the way of truth.
If you want to live, die in love.
Die in love if you want to remain alive.

JALALUDDIN RUMI

We can be born consciously, we can make love consciously and we can die consciously – three possibilities. All three are dependent upon one thing: breath. An animal (including the animal within us) cannot breathe consciously. Its instinct changes its breathing rate. Man and woman have the possibility of breathing consciously. We can literally awaken and work with breath every day of our lives. What is more, unless we awaken to the breath, we are not conscious. We can be so led astray by phenomena – physical, mental, emotional and psychic – that we cannot breathe. We need to build the observer so that the breath becomes conscious and not merely instinctive.

All the spiritual studies, techniques, exercises, visions and plans cannot come into being without breath. It simply is not possible. Consider a baby that is born in gentleness. It is already 'breathing' in the womb of the mother with the heartbeat of the mother, which is in the womb of the moment. We are in exactly that position. There is the heartbeat of the Divine Mother in this moment of time. And we are being breathed, though we have forgotten what that means.

Death is a tyrant. But we must always keep death in mind. Although we have much to endure in life, it is nothing compared with dying. We are born on the breath, and we apparently die on the breath. In the moment of death, if we are asleep in breath, we die asleep. But if we are awake, it is said that we are born into eternal life. What are we here for? To become responsible human beings. All else means nothing. We can die consciously in breath. As we breathe in, all and everything is contained in that moment, and as we breathe out, all and everything settles into the place of knowledge. Our life is only important relative to the degree of our responsibility within God and all that this means. Without breath we cannot learn.

We can choose the quality of air we breathe. That quality is dependent entirely upon our degree of awareness. Each of us is "a cosmic apparatus for the transformation of subtle energies" (G.I. Gurdjieff). That is what we are, a cosmic apparatus, and that is what we have to learn to be, through working with breath.

There has to be a rhythm of breath because there is a rhythm of the universe. The rhythm I work with is called the Mother's Breath. It is a sacred rhythm, 7-1-7-1-7, that corresponds to the octave in music. In the Mother's Breath, we breathe gently into the solar plexus for a count of seven, pause for one count, then breathe out from the centre of the chest for a count of seven. It is as if you were a lighthouse, radiating love and goodwill to all mankind in six directions.

Through conscious breath we receive the energies that God offers us every moment of our lives. If we do not take breath consciously, it is not surprising that we do not have the energy to make a commitment. If God made man in His Image, then man can be conscious to breathe in from the six directions and from all the different kingdoms. If we breathe in from all directions and accept what God has given us, then we have the energy to make a commitment. Otherwise it is often a quasi-commitment. It is not real. The commitment may not go through.

Commitment cannot be real without breath balanced both ways: in and out. Most of us never breathe out at all. We breathe in ("Wow!"), or we get caught in the world of attraction (inward sigh, "Oh!"). Our breath stops, right? Breath stops totally. We must learn to balance the in-breath by breathing out as well. We have to know when we are meant to be breathing *in* and when we are meant to be breathing *out*, on many levels.

Often we say we are going to do something, yet we never complete it. Life is what we have to complete because God gave us the possibility of completion in life. How can we possibly help other human beings unless we lead them, to the best of our ability, towards completion?

It is attention to breathing that is important. Every day, always try to take a little bit of time to breathe consciously. If we are going to become healers, conscious breath is vital. In the inner work our heartbeat changes through the breath. Therefore, try to take a little bit of time every day to pay attention to the breath. Never presume that our breath is always going to be given to us, because one day it might be taken away.

❧

The World Breathes Within You

Nikos Kazantzakis

What is your goal? To struggle and to cling firmly
to a branch, either as a leaf or flower or fruit, so that
within you the entire tree may move and breathe
and be renewed.

It is not you who calls. It is not your voice calling
from within your ephemeral breast. It is not only
the white, yellow and black generations of man calling
in your heart. The entire earth, with her trees and
her waters, with her animals, with her men and
her gods, calls from within your breast.
Earth rises up in your brains and sees her entire
body for the first time.

I recall an endless desert of infinite and flaming
matter. I am burning! I pass through immeasurable,
unorganized time, completely done, despairing,
crying in the wilderness. And slowly the flame subsides,
the womb of matter grows cool, the stone comes alive,
breaks open, and a small green leaf uncurls into the air,
trembling. It clutches the soil, steadies itself, raises
its head and hands, grasps the air, the water, the light,
and sucks at the universe. It sucks at the universe
and wants to pass it through its body – thin as
a thread – to turn it into flower, fruit, seed.
To make it deathless.

Immerse yourself in this vision with patience,
with love and high disinterestedness, until slowly
the world begins to breathe within you, the embattled
begin to be enlightened, to unite in your heart and
to acknowledge themselves as brothers.

ॐ

Hollow Breathing

A Practice

THIS IS A NICE LITTLE PRACTICE: ALL YOU HAVE TO DO
is to lie on your back and imagine – but don't be too
serious about it – that you are completely hollow. This
hollowness, really, is your body of light. Now breathe and
just try to see where you are *not* hollow. You may have a
pain in your stomach or someplace else, but this is not
what is meant here. You probably will find places where
you are not *hollow.* It is like going into a room with puffs
of clouds.

I had to do it like this when I was very ill and it was impossible for me to move, and so I learned it. So, wherever
you find it is not hollow, just breathe into that place with
light. Very seldom you will find the place where it is not
hollow to be where you expected it to be. And then, after a
while, suddenly you will find that you feel hollow again.

It won't last, but it is a lovely feeling of non-existence.
Actually, this hollowness is always here, but clouds do
come in sometimes.

ॐ

Breathe Into Me

Jalaluddin Rumi

There is some kiss we want with our whole lives,
    the touch of Spirit on the body.
Seawater begs the pearl to break its shell.
And the lily – how passionately it needs some wild
    darling!
At night, I open the window and ask the moon
    to come and press its face against mine.
Breathe into me.
Close the language-door and open the love-window.
The moon won't use the door, only the window.

ॐ

Being Awake

Inattention is what separates us from God.

IF WE ARE FULL OF INTERNAL ARGUMENTS, IF OUR
emotions control our life, if we are still causing pain to
others, if we are so narrow-minded that we cannot see that
breath is not limited by walls and if we cannot find ways to
overcome all these limitations, then it is time to wake up.
Once we become humble enough to realize that, until
we wake up and become conscious, we are just "machines",

84

to use Gurdjieff's expression, we set foot on a wonderful and joyful way to look at life.

Breathing is something you *have* to do, otherwise you would be dead. The thing is, mostly we *are* dead, but we think we are alive. Every time you are awake to the breath, you will wake yourself up to life. Every time you forget the breath, you are liable to be 'taken over' by the demanding self, that part of us which does not *want* to know.

The more I researched into this, the more I found – since, ultimately, breath and Spirit are one, and breath is life – what an incredible responsibility it is to wake up in order to become more conscious. But what a challenge it is to be present at every breath.

One day breath will stop. And then, at that point, it will be a question of whether we are awake and what we are awake to. In my second book, titled *To Know We're Loved*, John on his deathbed was awake to the words "I love you" (that means the whole of His Creation), "there is nothing else." That was pretty far ahead, certainly far ahead of me. Because to be able to say this and be fully conscious of it the very moment you die, would mean you have no negative emotions at that time whatsoever, no resentment, no envy, no pride and all that comes out of those three walls that separate us.

Imagine what it would feel like if you were in this situation right now. Use creative imagination. Remember every breath, i.e. place your attention on each breath and be aware of your presence. Inattention is what separates us from God. The more one is conscious of one's breath, the stronger is one's inner life. Once we are fully awake, that what lies within every breath is unfolded in each and every moment. The great Sufi Muhyiddin Ibn Arabi once said,

"All is contained in the Divine Breath like the day in the morning's dawn."

Surely the challenge here is that we sacrifice our personal will, that we become willing instruments to the Divine Will and thus the Divine Breath. This sacrifice requires of us to maintain such an inward collective state that our attention cannot wander for the duration of a single breath. After all, we do not know if at the end of this very breath we will be still alive. So it is necessary to remember ourselves in all situations, observe what is going on and, thus, build in our being what is called "the permanent I". You could also say "the permanent eye".

What does it mean to be an observer, and what does it mean to be a witness? Something does happen when you are awake to the breath. After a while, if you observe the breath and you have allowed the thought forms to go, there comes a time when you are being breathed, in which case you haven't the slightest idea whether you are breathing in or breathing out. Then you are in fact manifesting the observer. In an even higher state, you become the witness, the living witness of the Divine Presence.

But you never know when this will happen. Don't try to achieve it. Don't separate spiritual searching from normal life. Without inner work on the breath and without breathing to the best of our ability, we can be filled with information, even with what might be called "knowledge". But will we be in a state of knowing, and will we be a true witness of the Divine?

❧

Self

KATHLEEN RAINE

Who am I, who
Speaks from the dust,
Who looks from the clay?

Who hears
For the mute stone,
For fragile water feels
With finger and bone?

Who for the forest breathes the evening,
Sees for the rose,
Who knows
What the bird sings?

Who am I, for the sun fears
The demon dark,
In order holds
Atom and chaos?

Who out of nothingness has gazed
On the beloved face?

Recognition and Spirit

*Recognition brings the breath to bear
upon the face of the earth.*

IT WOULD BE ARROGANT TO SAY THE AVERAGE PERSON

is not alive at all, but it is true to say that, in most cases, only their animal nature is alive. The soul, lying dormant in the wonderful world of possibility, needs to be awakened. It is like the sleeping princess in the famous legends. The soul needs to be recognized. But by whom? The animal nature with its normal instinctual self, comprised only of the five senses as we know them, cannot recognize the soul.

The average person is captivated by a dead concept of life. Because we are ruled by attraction, we do not feel it is important to breathe consciously. Nowadays we have hugely advanced technology, and we are able to accomplish incredibly immense material achievements throughout the world. But without man learning about the art and science of breath, the elements will one day walk over us.

This, however, is not what they want to do. Rather the elements want to be recognized. You can read it in the Bible, in the Koran, in any of the sacred scriptures: we have all the elements within us. Whenever a man or a woman recognizes the elements, just like when woman and man recognize each other, something profound can happen. Picture to yourself, for instance, how at different times of history the world has almost been eradicated by the elemental forces. Can you imagine the loneliness of these elements, too? How they seem to say, "Look! See! I am here. I will serve you, I will give you everything, if only you recognize me."

Re-cognition means "to see again". Recognition brings the breath to bear upon the face of the earth. Recognition of the elemental kingdom gives us the power (not a personal power, but an ultimate power in humility) that if we say it will be, it will be.

But this is not possible without the knowledge of breath, without being able to 'walk on top of the breath'. This is why in the Sufi tradition it is said that if Jesus had even had more faith, he would not just have walked on water, he would have walked on air. To be on top of the breath is to be on top of time. You can have time in your hand, you can even literally be able to create time – but only with the knowledge of the breath and the added 'substance' of sound.

Sound fixes pattern. "In the beginning was the Word, and the Word was with God, and the Word was God." Through breath and sound the elements can become your friends. They befriend you, and you can ask them to go here or there, and they will. All we need to do is recognize the elements, and they will respond. If we are not willing or neglecting to recognize them, if we just don't care, we may have disasters like fires, earthquakes, hurricanes and floods both on a global and on a personal scale. All this is but an aspect of the Divine, of the one Lord, of the one God crying out saying, "Look at Me, I will help you if only you recognize Me."

If people don't wake up to listen to this call for recognition, who knows, maybe another flood will be unavoidable. Therefore we should start to train ourselves in breathing, and I am convinced we should even start to train our children from an early age on. Without knowing the art of breath, life can become cheap instead of valuable. And life should never be cheap.

When through our recognition the elements become – not our servants but – our friends and when man and women come together in recognition, we have what is called "the golden age" or "the new age" or whatever expression you prefer. So, never separate the Divine Kingdom and all the other kingdoms from mankind. Never separate these worlds, because they all are longing to be recognized, to come together and to serve.

Allow the descent of the purified forces, the *Ruh Allah,* which is Christ, the Spirit of God, to enter you. All you have to do is take a deep breath and breathe out as if it were your last breath. Let your whole body be filled with the *Ruh Allah* and remember to take all the gifts that God gives us. Take it from the earth, take it from the sky, from the front, from behind, from both sides. Breathe in all the beauty of the mineral kingdom. The elements will actually go to the right places if we breathe in gratefully.

Who is taking the breath if breath and Spirit are one? When we turn totally to God, as Jesus did, Mary did and every prophet has done, when you are ready and the time is right and you turn totally to God, breath and Spirit are one. That is the secret of prayer. And that is why Jesus, in our tradition, in the essence of Sufi teaching, is one of the Names for *Ruh Allah,* the Spirit of God.

What did Jesus say to his disciples? He did not say, "Pray in my name." He said, "Pray as I do." The word he used is phonetically spelled *alaha.* In "Allah" you got another l, but it is the same word. Is that not interesting? And it also means "breath". When you know this, you may eventually understand and see that there is no difference between breath and Spirit. They are not separate, because the Spirit is carried by the breath.

So, in the knowledge that breath and Spirit are one, the conscious breath of a conscious human being spreads the message of universal love beyond time and space, as we know it, forever.

Breathe On Me

Edwin Hatch

Breathe on me, Breath of God,
Fill me with life anew,
That I may love what Thou dost love,
And do what Thou wouldst do.

Breathe on me, Breath of God,
Until my heart is pure,
Until with Thee I will one will,
To do and to endure.

Breathe on me, Breath of God,
Blend all my soul with Thine,
Until this earthly part of me
Glows with Thy Fire Divine.

Breathe on me, Breath of God,
So shall I never die,
But live with Thee the perfect life,
Of Thine Eternity.

Time

*Every conscious breath we take
is the beginning of time.*

"TIME IS THE ETERNAL ATTRIBUTE OF GOD," AS A
Sufi saying goes. To this I would add, "And the secret of
eternal life is in the moisture on the breath." These are
some ideas to help you dig deeper into the mystery of time.

What is time? Let us try and look at it intelligently and
see how it relates to energy. First, we have this thing I call
"natural time", which is something we cannot really avoid,
so to speak, like life as such. If you committed suicide, life
as such goes on and so does natural time. But then, there is
the time that is created with every single breath we take,
particularly with the out-breath. If we live in expectation,
we will create an atmosphere of expectation – and time
changes. If we have negative or positive thinking, we will
block the flow and we will nearly always land up judging
the situation or somebody else or ourselves or whatever –
and time changes. Every time we are having opinions
about this and that and are haunted by thoughts, we are
broadcasting them – and time changes. We have to be
responsible for what we broadcast with every breath.
Because energy follows thought, we are wasting energy
whenever we are not conscious on the breath. And thus we
are wasting time and energy and life itself. But life is so
valuable! It is the only one we have got.

You have to understand that every conscious breath we
take is the beginning of time. What, then, could this mean

for the idea of conscious evolution? Love is the First Cause; "I was a Hidden Treasure and I loved to be known, so I created the world that I might be known," it says in a famous hadith of the prophet Muhammad (peace and blessing be upon him). When love flows through you in your out-breath, every conscious breath is a new beginning. But do not expect to experience the Big Bang every time you breathe out. No, it all happens step by step, *"ya wash ya wash"* as they say in Turkish. Nevertheless, it is better to be prepared. Just like it is better to spend a lot of time preparing to do your prayers than to just do them quickly and say, "That's done, now what's next?".

Never presume time. Watch it, but never presume it. Remember, this is the only time, the only life, you have in this world. Therefore we respect age as we respect and love the children, because we are all interconnected through innumerable threads of time, through dimension and dimension of time on so many levels, starting from that one dimensionless point I call "the *eternal beginning* of our lives". If you 'walk on the sands of time', remember all those who have gone before you and the sacrifices that have been made so that you are here, now. How many visible and invisible beings, wherever in our world, have helped, for instance, to make it possible for you to hold this book in your hands and read these lines at this very moment in time? What reservoirs of wish, what reservoirs of hope, belief and faith have been opened to bring you here in the arms of destiny? Listen to them on your breath. Listen to the children on your breath, listen to the old people on your breath, listen to your parents and grandparents and ancestors on your breath. They all long for recognition – now.

How long is time? Only as long as you are alive. The rest is history or illusion. And you are alive only as long as you are alive on the breath. History will repeat itself, but the effect of one conscious breath from one realized human being is said to go on for at least two hundred years. I wonder whether or not Jesus, when he walked on the water, was counting his rhythm of breath. The esoteric meaning of "walking on water" is "being on top of the breath" – because breath is full of moisture. If you are on top of the breath, you are on top of time. Then time is on your side and you are in the arms of destiny and not in the hands of fate.

If you are conscious on the breath and if you have learned to properly visualize what you are going to do, you are creating time yourself. Not the flow of natural time, but the time that you are responsible for. One day, as you develop and learn more, you will even be able to visualize your own death. Not the time of it. But you will be able to visualize it as merely a transition, nothing more. A transition in which you leave behind fear, resentment, pride and all the other protective shields of your "poor me".

Time is not what you think it is. If we are asleep to life, how can we know that breath is life? The secret of eternal life is in the moisture on your own breath. So 'walk on the moisture of your breath,' which is like 'walking on the wings of time'. Then, and only then, you can humbly stand proud and, through the present moment, help the Divine Qualities manifest from the unmanifest, so that the world to come can walk into the space that you have helped create in beauty. "Walk in the beauty of your children," as the Navajo Indians say in their *Blessed Beauty Prayer*. Within us, there is something called "pure time", which is the eternal beginning. One day, God willing, we receive a taste of this, and then we become thirsty and we want to go to the source. Nothing less will do, because then we know that we can be of service as we have become truly conscious human beings.

I want you to learn to respect time, because if you respect time, you may learn something about life. Therefore I try to transmit to you, again and again, the sacredness of breath, which *is* life. Once you know without any shadow of a doubt that this is the only life you have, then – within this beauty of time, because time *can* be beautiful – you may come to know yourself.

⁊

It Was Now

Ilse Middendorf

Actually, there are no limits. There are only transitions. Limits are much too hard.

To find your own rhythm, this is the most important thing. Once you find it, you are at home.

If you want to find your rhythm, you need patience.

Out-breath is expression.

If you take a breath *now*, was that before or after?
Is it now? It was not before, it was not after, it was *now*.

The Womb of the Moment

The time of the beloved Virgin Mary is not just
a historical event. When is it not?

AGAIN AND AGAIN I HAVE TOLD THE PEOPLE WHO
studied with me over the past forty years the story of
Hazrati Maryam, the Virgin Mary, and how the esoteric
meaning of the virgin birth, and many inner secrets concerned with this event, are given to us in the holy Koran
and in the teachings of the Sufi masters, such as the Sheikh
al-Akhbar, Muhyiddin Ibn Arabi. It would be foolish
indeed to merely read this story and then put down the
books as though we have finally understood it, once and
for all!

The meaning goes on and on unfolding with each conscious breath a student takes for the sake of his or her love
of God – not just for themselves. What a mistake that
would be, and how often do we forget to remember!
Anyway, for those who haven't heard it yet, here is the
story, but in my own paraphrasing.

Once, when Mary was alone in her room and as pure as
the day she was born, there was a knock on the door. She
was frightened. She knew that she was meant to be alone,
and did not know of anyone who would be coming to
visit. Perhaps her family was away, out of the house.

Again there was knocking, and then a man opened the
door. He was the most beautiful man she had ever seen,
so much so that the sight of such beauty almost took her
breath away.

At that moment, the story continues, she turned totally to her Lord. The man smiled, radiant with light, and said, "Do not worry, Mary. I am Gabriel, the Messenger of the Lord. I have come to give you a message of good news."

It was the moment of the Annunciation. Mary, now realising intuitively who this beautiful man was, relaxed. And at that very moment Gabriel blew into her the Spirit of God, *Ruh Allah.* Thus, Jesus is known to be not only the saviour, the healer, a prophet in the Line of the Prophets, but also the Spirit, the Christ, who will come again to raise us to the truth – the truth that, God willing, *insh' Allah,* we may all experience individually and in our own unique ways. We will even understand *in our own language.*

It is also said – and here is another important piece of news – that if Mary had not relaxed at that moment, Jesus would have been impossible to live with due to his *uncompromising nature.*

I will leave it to you to look deep inside your heart to find the many meanings within this story. However, I will give you a hint as to just one of them. What could it mean if I say that "ever since the time of the Virgin Mary, there is no more need to think"? Did not God say in the Bible, "Fear not, for I have come to grant you a child who will bring great joy to you and to all mankind" (Luke 2.10)?

The *time* of the beloved Hazrati Maryam, the Virgin Mary, is not just a historical event of two thousand years ago! When is it *not?* When will we learn?

Perhaps it may also interest you to know that, in the inner circles, it is said that the word which Gabriel *breathed* into Mary at the moment of the Annunciation comes from the Aramaic root *bsr,* which, translated into Arabic, is the word *beshara.* Its meaning in English is "good news".

ॐ

A Spirit of God

MUHYIDDIN IBN ARABI

The Spirit (*Ruh*) [that is to say Christ] was manifested
   by the water of Mary and the breath of Gabriel,
In the form of a man made of clay,
In the purified body of [corruptible] nature that
   he calls "prison";
So that he is staying there since more than
   a thousand years.
A 'Spirit of God', of no other:
It is for that that he resuscitated the dead and
   created the bird from clay.
His relation towards his Lord is such,
That he acts through it in superior and inferior worlds.
God purified his body and elevated him in spirit,
And made of him the symbol of His Act of creation.

ॐ

The Breath of God's Mercy

A Sufi is called "the son of the moment".

"LET ME TELL YOU A LITTLE ABOUT THE INNER MEANING
of the Virgin Mary before we arrive at her chapel." Hamid
seemed determined to push me into some sort of realization.

"You must first of all understand that although I seem to
be talking about a historical event, everything of which I
speak is within you and is happening *at this moment*. There
is no other; and what happened, in our world, two thousand years ago is part of the unfoldment of this moment,
not *that* moment but this very instant. It is neither a question of looking back two thousand years nor of trying to
recapture the moment in your imagination. All you have
to do is to be awake. Be awake in this moment within
yourself, and it will be your own understanding. It may
take time to unfold in our world, but the truth, and the
unfoldment of the truth, are always there."

He paused and was silent for so long that my mind
began to wander – to the remains of our breakfast, to the
proposed trip to Ephesus, to the state of repair of the car.
Finally he leaned forward in his chair and looked at me
searchingly. "I want you to listen to me carefully," he said.
"Make your mind quiet and just listen.

"Your body is the Virgin Mary. The Spirit is Christ, the
Word that was conveyed through Gabriel, the eternal
messenger. The breath is the breath of the Mercy of God,
and it is that breath that quickens the soul. Until the soul
is quickened by the Spirit it is like an unfledged bird.

99

"There are many paths to God, but the way of Mary is the sweetest and most gentle. If you can melt into Mary, the matrix, the blueprint of life, the Divine Mother, you will be formed and shaped in Christ and Christ in you, and thus through the breath of God's Mercy you will come into being and know Him. For it is the breath of mercy that bestows being. Every moment God appears in living form, never manifesting Himself twice in the same moment.

"Mary brought Jesus into the world because she was chosen to be the one for this work, and so she was trained in the knowledge of birth. It is said that Gabriel, the messenger, appeared to Mary in the form of a man. She thought that he wanted her as a woman, so she froze for a moment, turning to her Lord. If she had not relaxed, then the child born from that moment would have been uncompromising and impossible to live with. Your body is the Virgin Mary, the Spirit is Christ, the breath is the breath of God's Mercy. Your soul remains asleep until it is quickened by the Holy Spirit. Each moment of our lives a child is born somewhere. The child that is born could be a God-conscious human being, or it could be uncompromising, in endless competition with life. The responsibility in the realization of these things is immense. If you can hear what I am saying to you now, then you will begin to understand. As you are permeated with the Spirit, you may, *insh' Allah,* begin to know, but it will not make life easier or lighter for you. It may make life heavier, but heavier with meaning and purpose.

"Mary is the Divine Mother. Mary is in the blue of the flame, and Mary is the matrix of all Divine Possibility in form, here, in our world. It is necessary that she be recognized. Learn to love God with all of your being, every part of yourself, your heart, your mind, your soul, and then we may all be granted the understanding of the meaning of the virgin birth. Learn to pray and your prayers will come back from the very matrix that forms the child.

"A Sufi is called 'the son of the moment'. As you melt each moment into Mary, something is being redeemed that a child may be born, and what is being born is the son of the moment. That child may become God-realized and thus be called a Sufi, or he may walk the earth unaware, asleep – not yet human, not conscious of God or of the wonders of His Creation, having no knowledge of himself and thus no real understanding of love. Your body is the Virgin Mary – remember this each moment of your life. This is the responsibility that we must take as we come into knowledge, into being.

"Mary was chosen to bear Jesus because she kept her purity intact. Simple people call this her 'virginity', but those who know understand that to be pure means to be completely adaptable, to flow with each moment, to be like a running stream cascading from the waters of life itself. To be pure is to spread joy, and joy is the unfoldment of the knowledge of the Perfection of God. The 'Work' that you have been searching for is the Spirit of God, and the Spirit of God is the Christ, which comes to redeem the world. The eternal messenger is always within, waiting to unfold the moment through the Word, and one day when Mary is recognized again, there will be a reappearance of the Christ, manifested in the outer world. Remember who Mary is, and one day, when you are ready, and when God so wills it, you will know what I have told you."

Faith with Proof

Hazrat Inayat Khan

For the mystic, breath is not only a science, but the knowledge of breath is mysticism; and mysticism to the thinker is both science and religion. The mystery of breath is not a thing that can be comprehended by the brain only. The principles of mysticism rise from the heart of man. They are learned by intuition and proved by reason. This is not only faith, though it is born of faith: it is faith with proof.

❦

7-1-7 Breathing

A Practice

SIT IN A HARD-BACKED CHAIR. KEEPING YOUR BACK straight, without forcing it, will allow the flow of energy to move as it should. With practice, your back will straighten naturally.

Place your feet flat on the floor, with heels close together and toes apart forming a triangle. The legs should be uncrossed. The arms should be relaxed and if possible in an unstressed position; the hands should rest on the knees.

The solar plexus has two subsidiary centres, which are located in the knees. The knees are highly sensitive instruments. If you focus your attention on your knees while blindfolded, you can sense that the knees send out a beam of energy. You will not walk into a wall due to the inner sense that comes from the area of your knees.

Do this practice for about *ten minutes* and no longer. It can be done several times a day with safety.

All of these practices are to help us to see God's Beauty and to live beautiful lives. Before you start the conscious breathing practice, visualize the most beautiful object in nature you can imagine. It could be a plant, a tree, a waterfall, the sea or whatever means something real to you.

For this practice, the eyes can be open or closed. Either way, focus on a point approximately eight feet in front of you. If your eyes are closed, then put the picture of whatever you have chosen in front of you through visualization. If you are focussing on an object, put it as close to eight feet away from you as you can. *Do not meditate on a candle* in this practice. This is very important. The object of the visualization is to help you focus your attention, not to meditate on the object itself.

Now we come to this sacred rhythm, this 7-1-7-1-7 rhythm of the Mother's Breath, about which I have written in former books and which I have been teaching for so long. The rhythm came from ancient Egypt, and there are many hieroglyphics showing how this practice, and others, are done.

The method is simple though initially it may seem difficult, since we are used to just breathing without any form of attention or consciousness. You are going to breathe into the solar plexus for the count of seven, pause for one count, and then for another seven counts radiate out breath from the "heart centre", as we call the point in the centre of the chest. You may notice that the rhythm corresponds exactly to the octave in music. Please remember that it is not the speed that counts, be it slow or relatively fast. It is the actual number of counts that we are talking about. Choose the speed that suits you.

First, find a point in the centre of your solar plexus area, and also the heart centre. Breathe into the solar plexus for the count of seven and from fourteen directions simultaneously, from in front and behind, from above and below, from left and right as well as from the remaining eight diagonals. As you breathe, bring in all the elements of the earth, the minerals – You can even breathe in vitamins by choice if you wish! – and fill yourself with all that the body and its subtle counterparts need. Do not be embarrassed about taking what you need in the understanding that all this is done in the name of service.

Having breathed in for the count of seven, pause for one count and at the same time bring your attention to the centre of the chest. Then breathe out for the count of seven. As you breathe out, radiate love and goodwill to all mankind from the centre of the chest in the same fourteen directions, as if you are a lighthouse for the ships that are entering the harbour.

At this point, there is a tremendous sense of wonder and gratitude in the realization that, indeed, we are able to serve our fellow human beings and the planet itself.

To complete the practice, return to the senses. As in other practices, feel your body and take responsibility for it once more. Be awake to the room or the surroundings, and finally agree that you have fulfilled what you set out to do.

We can choose the quality of the air that we breathe. As you progress, through correct visualization, you can breathe the air that is circulating in certain sacred areas of the planet without leaving the chair upon which you are sitting.

The last step in the practice, which, after all, is an alchemical process, is the refining of the breath. Begin taking only us much breath as you actually need and are given. This should require as little effort as the fluttering of a butterfly's wings. There is no more need to force the breath. In a sense, at this stage, you are not breathing. Rather, you are being breathed.

Breath is life! This is the still point in a waiting world.

❧

Universe Is Given Life

Joseph Rael

We are all music. With each inhalation we identify
our purpose to be alive, vibrations of the here and now,
and our universe is created. And with each exhalation,
the universe is given new life. This is how we create
the future; what we choose to live in each and every
moment resonates outward on our breath. We inhale
in one moment, and we are presentness; we exhale
in the next, and we are futureness.

❧

Nourishment

Without remembering breath as often as you can,
you are missing one of those foods that are necessary
to build the body of resurrection.

THE AIR THAT WE BREATHE AND OUR IMPRESSIONS

are among the most important kinds of food we have. When we breathe unconsciously, we just get what we need to keep alive. But when we breathe consciously, when we breathe with awareness, we receive and digest the finer substances the air has to give and we nourish body and soul at the same time. In order to be able to refine and digest this nourishment for our own good and for the good of others, we need, first of all, to be grateful and without judgment.

How many people do you meet on this so-called spiritual path, under whatever label, who have opinions. Because they are so full of views and attitudes, so full of judgement, they cannot transform their food. They are unable to distil nourishment from their impressions because they won't open themselves up to the truth of the moment, to the truth as it is now. And so they run the risk of starving to death.

You will never "die before you die" if you are starving to death. If you are not grateful, you won't die before you die, you will simply starve. The fuller you are with the Love of God, which is also in the impressions and in the air you breathe, the more easily you can die before you die.

Without remembering breath – that breath is life and that we are all sharing the same air – as often as you can, you are missing one of those foods that are necessary to build the first 'inner body', which Gurdjieff calls the *Kesdjan* body. In esoteric Christian terms, particularly in Eastern Orthodox Christianity, it is called "the body of resurrection". This inner body – which as a matter of fact is only the beginning of a further body called "the higher being body" – we simply cannot build without being grateful for life and being aware of the breath.

We have within us certain means for accumulation, for which I use the word "reservoir" as a symbol. What is a reservoir? It is obviously a sort of container like, for example, a water reservoir. Such a reservoir needs to be filled in order that the water can be given out to the land so that there is always enough to keep things basically in balance. If it is not properly filled when there is a drought, the reservoir dries up, the water gets full of algae, the fish die and there is no power. It is the same inside of us. Only, *our* reservoirs are filled with breath or Spirit. And the way in which we can fill them is through *sensing*.

By extending your attention, your consciousness, and by employing what we call "pure memory", you can breathe in all the qualities and the elements you need from anywhere. Pure memory is like pure beauty. Most memory we have is in comparison, isn't it? We have a memory of something beautiful, but we also can remember something ugly. There is always an opposite to it somewhere. Pure memory, however, is different. As we become more conscious, we can apply pure memory and, through refinement, transform it into a certain type of food which is necessary. If, for example, you were in the middle of smog in Los Angeles and you were trying to breathe in deeply, how could you refine the breath? The answer is: through pure memory, because you are not limited by space and time; you only *think* you are. Through pure memory, we can take the air from a pure place. The late John G. Bennett called it "conscious stealing", because in pure memory you can 'go' to a sacred spot and you can breathe from that place without moving. There are many sacred spots on the planet, like Mount Kailash in Tibet for instance. Or you may have your own special spots. It could be a certain tree; a tree loves to be recognized. You can always breathe from such a spot and refine the air.

However, when trying to do this, you must be awake and attentive. As long as you watch the breath, you can let your creative imagination bring in these beautiful pictures and fill the reservoirs with the sense of beauty. But if you forget your breath, imagination can easily turn into fantasy, wishful thinking and sentimentality – and that is much too low a level. It is very easy to fall back into sentimentality. The key word is *beauty*. "The sole purpose of love is beauty."

As long as you breathe consciously, you can take in all the gifts that God gives us. Among them are the elements of fire, earth, air and water. If you breathe in gratefully, these elements will be refined to the necessary level of nourishment and actually go to the right places to fill up your reservoirs (see the Reservoir Practice, page 119). When you breathe out, then radiate out the breath, the Spirit, in the form of light. This is the light which is not opposite to darkness; it is the light of understanding, the light of wisdom, the light of friendship. Remember, concrete walls will not stop the breath. The floor will not stop the breath. And when you let down your own walls, the walls of resentment, envie and pride, nothing will stop the breath of love.

With *fire,* do not visualize flames but rather the quality of the heat of the sun. Psychologically or emotionally you can think of kindness, of warmth, of all that is beautiful. This inner fire produces light and transforms the residue, the "dross", as we call it in alchemy. There are many ways to breathe in this warmth. For instance, I always visualize a line of light coming from the sun. Replenish, refill your reservoirs with this element of fire. If you do it correctly, there is often a tremendous feeling of joy and warmth, just as if dawn had come again and the world, for today, is going to be okay. Sometimes I, personally, feel I want to move and dance because of this joy. As you know, high emotions like this usually are very catching and may be beneficial for everybody.

As for the element of *earth,* remember your earth connectedness and breathe in all the aspects of earth. Breathe in the beauty of the mineral kingdom, the vegetable kingdom, all the different Kingdoms of God. You can breathe in every single mineral on this planet. If you visit a sacred spot somewhere, you can sense the real pure memory that is still in the crystals in the ground. In Australia, for example, the Aborigines have been there forty thousand years; but you don't have to leave your room to be able to breathe in the elements of earth from there. What does the earth mean to *you?* The trees, the plants, everything? We *live* on the earth. If we remember this, we cannot *not* have a sense of gratefulness; we just feel grateful. We are giving life to our earth, to the earth elements within us.

With the element of *air,* breathe in the finest air you can imagine. Again, you do not have to leave your room or the place where you are. You can actually bring it to you; let pure memory help you. You can remember the finest mountain air from anywhere in the world. For me, it will always be the air on the west coast of Scotland. But we all have our personal ideas or feelings of what pure air is like. You know what air, oxygen, does to water. If one puts air into the reservoir, the water gets better in every way and the fish life becomes abundant. Remember that we are eighty-five percent water.

And so we come to the element of *water*. Breathe in pure water. Wherever you go now, people are finally realising that water, really, is the greatest commodity on planet earth. Try to choose the purest water you can find, water as it should be. We all thirst for it, don't we? Remember the beauty of water, the movement of water, the stillness of water. Through conscious choice and loving attention we can transform the water in ourselves.

When you breathe in all these elements and all other qualities which may be needed, always be *absolutely selfish* and remember that God gives us everything. And when you breathe out, be *absolutely unselfish;* offer it back and share it. In other words, don't suck it in to be powerful, don't do it for yourself. It is all a question of remembrance and then to give it back. Even a tree wants to share. At the same time, don't *project* it outside, don't be ambitious.

Be grateful that you are alive, and your out-breath will go in the right place because there is nothing outside of you. There is a lot that *appears* to be, but in reality there is nothing outside your arm span. So don't be frightened to fill up your own universe, your own worlds, on the out breath.

As you have to eat every day of your life, you can always spend ten, fifteen minutes a day consciously breathing in and breathing out and thus replenishing, refilling your reservoirs – for your own good, and for the good of others. In Christian terms we say, "My cup floweth over," don't we? That is the chalice. So, you can imagine that – if your reservoirs are full and if the hands are the extension of the heart – the chalice can be given to others.

❦

The Bridge

Hazrat Inayat Khan

It is the mystery of breath which shows the mystic
that life is not the material part of man's being,
but consists of the part of his being which is unseen.
Breath is the bridge between soul and body, keeping
the two connected, and the medium of their action
and reaction upon each other.

❦

Directions

*Any inner work to do with breath is helping
to make space for the world to come.*

YOU WILL SURELY UNDERSTAND THAT TO SIMPLY

read papers about breath and breathing, such as these discourses, and then put the book back on the shelf is not enough. Obviously, you will need a lot of daily practice and you will have to keep contemplating on the ideas I give you and the perspectives I teach. In order to understand, you will have to dig deep.

What could it mean, for instance, to breathe in "from different directions"? I say, you can breathe in from fourteen directions into the centre of your solar plexus. Of course there is more to it, much more, than just a geometrical picture in which you imagine yourself to be in the centre of the six directions from above and below, front and behind, left and right as well as from the eight additional diagonals. The deeper you can dig out the truth within these ideas, the more you can see why this breathing in from different directions can have a very transformative effect on you and, therefore, on the whole future of this planet. So let's have a closer look at some aspects of these directions and what they could actually mean and represent.

Any inner work to do with breath, and of course other practices such as Yoga, is helping to make space for the world to come. But the world to come, as my beloved teacher Bulent Rauf said, will come "when it will come,

not when you think it is going to come." It is very important we remember that. It is why we also say, "Patience
is the key to joy." We prepare the way, and we are our
own forerunner. These attitudes I believe to be vital in
any breathing practice. But you hardly ever read about
them and, in fact, in many cases a lot of the breathing
practices increase spiritual ambition, which does nobody
any good.

When I say, "Breathe in *from above* the head into the
solar plexus," it isn't just above the physical head. In some
esoteric schools they call it "sidereal energy", which means
the world of the stars, doesn't it? In other words, you are
breathing in from another dimension than the one we are
experiencing normally. When I was first taught this I was
very young, and I remember my then teacher saying to me,
"When you can be aware of the stars while the sun is still
shining, you will know what it means."

Breath has no limitations. Everything is given to us, and
we awaken it through love. The energy of the stars and the
planets is all for us, but we can walk along the road of life
and never be awake to the stars when the sun is shining.
By being actively receptive, attentive and in loving kindness, we can breathe in star energy from above. How do
you listen, for instance, to what a bird wants? You don't
force it, you *love* it so that *it* listens – and then you can
listen to what the bird wants. In the same way you can
imagine all this incredible star energy trickling down into
each one of us, and in love we can breathe it in.

We can breathe in the energy of the stars and the sun
and the planets, and no clouds get in our way, not even our
personal clouds. It is all given to support us, like it says in
the Koran [10:24 and 16:66],

as water which We send down so the herbage of the earth, of which men and cattle eat, grows luxuriantly thereby [...] And most surely there is a lesson for you in the cattle; We give you to drink of what is in their bellies [...] pure milk, easy and agreeable to swallow for those who drink.

And so we are given the milk and the leather and so many other things.

"From above", obviously, also has the symbolism of a world to come which is still in a formative state. "As above, so below." How can a formative world, which wants to enter, do so if we are not empty, if we still are full of judgments and so on? It is easy to see with parking angels, for example. When you ask a parking angel, you will get a parking space almost certainly – if you say "please" first and "thank you" afterwards. But if after a while you forget to say "thank you", the angels go somewhere else, because angels were all born with good manners. They just get bored and go away. It's simply about saying, "Please, can I have a parking space," and "thank you" because there is one.

When we speak about breathing in *from below,* through our feet, obviously, we are talking about breathing in earth energy. You may breathe in all the elements of the mineral kingdom and the vegetable kingdom which you feel or think you need. Actually you don't even have to think, because God knows your needs. Just be grateful that the knowledge is known and that we are all uniquely different and uniquely beautiful. Feel your connectedness to the earth. By breathing in from below, you give yourself a certain type of energy, a certain type of strength.

Always remember that breath is not limited by walls or floors. If you are sitting on top of six inches of concrete, it will make no difference. Don't be neither puritanical and small-minded nor sentimental about these things. You can sit on the 58th floor of a New York skyscraper and still breathe in from below the level of the subway. The earth is always 'underneath' your feet. It's only us and our sense of separation that makes us feel we have to be in some special place for this. Remember, "Wheresoe'er ye stand, there is holy ground." We have to learn to breathe consciously everywhere and all the time.

Now, breathing in *from behind* surely refers to the past. You are not walking backwards towards Christmas, are you? Mostly, we carry our past with us, just like a back-pack, and we are absolutely terrified of letting go. Rather like swallowing our teeth, we may forget what has happened in the past because we want to avoid looking at it. Every event can be seen in the relative sense as either positive or negative, can't it? What might be very positive to me is a disaster to you and vice versa. But we must not judge it – it is.

Thus, when bringing in "breathing from behind", the great key is not to judge. If we look at what we judge and who we judge, at what we judge to be "right" or "wrong" and so on, we can see how limited we are. Every religious leader, every spiritual teacher has said, in some words or other, that "thou shalt not judge." Scientifically, in modern psychology at least, it is relatively easy to explain why, and certainly so in mystical science. There is a famous saying, "You never know another person's name until their last breath." We spend our lives actually judging what we see, even the essence of another human being, pretending we can look at their inside. But the more we judge, the less we *can* see.

When you breathe in from behind, you are consciously taking the responsibility of awakening trapped energy. Trapped energy, here, is meant neither negatively nor positively. It is a question of awakening something by recognition. It is almost as though you give it life again, so there can be flow. When you breathe in from behind, you will awaken memories that perhaps you do not want to have. But we should try to be able to have a gentle sense of courage, every day, so that we don't go on collecting this trapped, hard, even crystal-like energy in our own fields, in our backpack so to speak.

All transformation takes place in and through the present moment. And there is no present moment without a conscious human being. When we breathe in, as if it were from behind ourselves, we are breathing in the past, both the unredeemed pain and the beauty, but not the one seen as ugly and the other seen as beautiful. Rather, we breathe in without judgement, bringing in all that has to be brought through back into the light. We respect and honour our parents and our ancestors – which is to be understood literally *and* figuratively – going back far beyond the time we can remember. "Honour thy father and thy mother that thou mayest live long on the earth." This way we are gratefully coming into being in the present moment.

Breathe in; let it come through. For me, there were always two words that have helped me survive: *gratefulness* and *forgiveness.* We all make mistakes; I have, more than most I expect. First of all be grateful that you have managed to bring something to your attention, because "gratefulness is the key to will." Then, without a sense of guilt, ask for forgiveness. Remember that "He is the All-Forgiver." Sooner or later that which traps that particular pattern will melt. But you have to trust, as it will not happen in the sequential time and the timing that we expect. You will never know when.

And so you breathe in from all directions, from above and below, from front and behind and from every other direction, transforming your own pain and your own fears, turning to the One Source. God willing, you will receive at this very moment the ingredient which will help you in this process. Take that ingredient. Once the energy is completely transformed, it is limitless.

Lastly, you bring your attention to the centre of the chest, the so-called "heart centre". And when you breathe out from there, again in all directions like a lighthouse, radiate out this energy which has been transformed into light and love. Breathe it out into a waiting world. Do not, however, project it out onto people. Like a river, it will go where it is needed. Somebody in China, or Russia or Bosnia may get it. Don't worry too much about the counting, just breathe in and out quietly. Be. From this state of being something can become, for "there is no creation in the relative world, there is only the becoming of being." Feel the Glory of God in your own heart. If you do this properly, there is a real cry of recognition in the world that God has given us. This is part of *dhikr,* of remembrance, when we see God and His Creation as *one.*

ঽ

Only Breath

Jalaluddin Rumi

Not Christian or Jew or Muslim, not Hindu,
Buddhist, Sufi or Zen. Not any religion

or cultural system. I am not from the East
or the West, not out of the ocean or up

from the ground, not natural or ethereal, not
composed of elements at all. I do not exist,

am not an entity in this world or the next,
did not descend from Adam and Eve or any

origin story. My place is placeless, a trace
of the traceless. Neither body or soul.

I belong to the beloved, have seen the two
worlds as one and that one call to and know,

first, last, outer, inner, only that
breath breathing human being.

Replenishing the Reservoirs

A Practice

ALL PRACTICES WHICH INVOLVE THE ART AND SCIENCE
of breath and breathing are based on the simple saying,
"Breath is life." Even repeating these words can have a profound effect on a person's well-being. For example, the
words could be repeated as "breath is *life*" or "breath *is*
life". The inner understanding in all the ancient traditions
is that – when we come to true understanding – breath and
Spirit are not separate. They are one and the same, but
only in the realization of the Divine Unity. Even the Sioux
Indians in the United States, with whom I have had much
contact, will say the same thing. In the Bible, the Torah
and the Koran, it is the same if you read carefully what is
explained.

This particular practice is really a *distillation* of over
forty years of training in meditation and different practices
which involve the breath. I have not mixed up Western and
Eastern practices, such as Hatha Yoga and Sufi practices,
but rather, after so much experience, have put together
a series of practices, useful for the Western culture and
mind, which is, after all, very different to either the Eastern
or the Middle Eastern approaches to psychology and spiri-
tuality.

The circulation of *chi* or Prana or the vital force, known
by many names in the different traditions, is essential for
our health, mental, psychological and physical. Visualization is also a very valuable tool, used together with this

practice. Of course, any practice has an underlying purpose, and that is to do with harmony, flow, peace and realization of the unity. As I said above, this is essentially a very simple practice, which requires little time; and yet, if worked with regularly, benefit can soon be felt. Regularity is essential.

From personal experience I can certainly say that, in the same way as the battery of a car needs to be kept charged, times will come for us all when we have allowed our reservoirs to become so depleted that special efforts need to be made to refill our batteries with this special energy. Normally I suggest that the practice only needs to be done about four times a day – after all, it only takes twelve sequences of conscious breaths to complete the cycle – but if you find your energy has dropped to a low ebb, due to illness or some other reason, then it is perfectly possible to practice this exercise several times a day. Naturally, it is better if we are in the open air, and the best times are always between 2 a.m. and 4 a.m. or at dawn, as well as noon and sunset. If, for some reason, you are unable to sit in a chair to complete this practice, then you can also do it lying down on your back in the most relaxed position you can. If there is somebody who can breathe with you at times of difficulty, perhaps holding your hands, then the stronger of the two people will help the weaker, but without being drained of their own Pranic energy.

I shall now describe how to work with this practice, written very simply. It is necessary to realize that you cannot *think* when you are practising. It is necessary to learn how to do it, memorize the method carefully, and then just *do it!* Do not ask for any reward; do not expect any specific results. Just complete the practice in and for love.

Always dedicate your inner work to the Highest, to God or whatever name you may have as your personal reality, before commencing, and say a prayer of gratefulness after you have really tried to complete the practice to the best of your ability. There is no success or failure in this inner work.

Sit in a chair with your back as straight as possible, but without any strain, and with your knees spread at a 45 degree angle. Your hands are on your knees in a relaxed manner. Face in the direction of the sun, i.e. towards east in the early morning, but follow the path of the sun during the day. Feel very *present* in your own body, relaxing tensions in key areas such as the shoulders and the neck.

Come into the rhythm of the Mother's Breath, i.e. the rhythm of 7-1-7-1-7, breathing in to the count of seven, with a short pause following the in-breath, and then breathing out to the count of seven and continuing after another pause. The breath should be taken from all fourteen directions – from in front and behind, from above and below, from left and right as well as from the remaining eight diagonals – down into the solar plexus area, and even lower into the belly, on the in-breath, then the attention is brought to the centre of the chest, and then the out-breath is *radiated out* in all fourteen directions from the chest area. For example, imagine your consciousness is right in the middle of a lighthouse by the sea at that time. Continue, gently and without effort, with this breathing rhythm at any speed which feels comfortable to you. Again, do not try too hard. It takes time to establish this rhythm, which, eventually, becomes almost like second-nature, following the musical law of the octave.

There are two very special areas in the subtle anatomy of man. Of course there are actually many, but, in this practice, we concentrate particularly on two areas which we call *the first* and *the second reservoir*. These are situated in the area behind the centre of the chest and in the centre of the brain. These areas can act as storage vessels for *chi,* Prana, the vital force, *élan vital* or whatever you wish to call it, and become activated by the breath, now realized to be one with the Spirit, but carried by the active attention to the breathing. They are connected to the different parts of the subtle anatomy of man through many different channels, including the acupuncture meridians. The advantages of knowing this are surely obvious in our daily lives.

Now you come to the actual discipline of the reservoir practice, which requires only three times four sequences of two conscious in- and out-breaths each. First of all, sitting upright on your chair, visualize a line of light stretching down through the top of your head from way, way above down through your spine, through the coccyx, into the ground, acting, as it were, like an anchor. Be deeply and gratefully aware of the ground under your feet, Mother Earth, and universes of pure light above. Be awake to the front of your body, stretching out into infinity, and also to what is 'behind' you, in the relative sense, also stretching way back. Our centre is in the middle of this imagined cross of light, coming and going in all directions – even lines of light coming in from all angles. It is as though you are in the centre of a light-crystal.

The **first four sequences** begin (1) by breathing into the solar plexus *from all directions*. This is done by putting your attention to the solar plexus and drawing in the breath, in the form of light from 'above', from 'below' from the earth, remembering all the wonderful minerals involved, and even the vegetable kingdom, from 'behind', bringing in all the as-yet unredeemed beauty hidden in past time, and from the 'front' from the world of wonderful possibilities, providing living hope for us all. Still on the in-breath, as you are drawing this light or energy into the solar plexus area, move your attention a bit lower into a point about two to three fingers width below the navel. Then there is the pause. On the out-breath (2) you now push the breath down into the coccyx, at the base of the spine, to the count of seven. Again there is a slight pause. Then (3) you breathe up into the *first reservoir,* the area behind the chest, filling, as it were, this reservoir with life force. Again a pause. On the out-breath (4) you radiate love and good-will to all mankind in all directions, like a lighthouse, as I explained previously. You do this part of the practice four times. It is enough.

In the **second four sequences** you repeat as above, but as you bring your breath up (3) into the first reservoir, now already filled, you move your breath *through it,* and on up through the spinal cord into the *second reservoir* in the centre of the brain, paying particular attention to the neck and base of the skull, where the energy can seem to get 'stuck'. If necessary, move your head from side to side to free this energy. When you find the second reservoir, you again fill it with light or energy, and then on the out-breath (4) you breathe out through what is sometimes called "the third eye", situated between the eye-brows, as though you were 'washing' this area with light. Again this part of the practice is just completed four times, and no more is desired or necessary. After these four sequences of carefully placed breaths, you have completed two cycles.

The **third four sequences** in the last part of the breathing practice are concerned with the words *flow* and *circulation*. Bringing your attention back to the centre of the chest, the heart centre, you *allow* the energy to circulate up the back of your body (with the in-breaths 1 and 3), and down the front (with the out-breaths 2 and 4), almost as though the body becomes the shape of an egg, lit by light, and with the life force circulating around, within and through it. Remain in this position, observing and allowing the flow to move through and around you, granting you harmony, peace and an inner strength and conviction which, in fact, is always with you, but which can become consciously activated through this practice. You could stay in this last stage of the practice, after the required four sequences, for a length of time that feels comfortable to you.

The eyes can be open or closed when you do this practice, dependent, of course, on the brightness of the sun. When you have completed your work, and if your eyes have been closed, open them carefully, being conscious of your body, in total gratefulness for all life, and repeat the words, "These are the eyes through which God sees; these are the ears through which God hears" and "There *is* only one Absolute Existence, one Absolute Being, and I (repeating your own name) am witness to this beauty."

Finally, in peace and gratefulness, get up from the chair consciously and go about the day's business.

ʔ⃛

Nowness

Chögyam Trungpa

In this kind of meditation practice, the concept
of nowness plays a very important part. In fact,
it is the essence of meditation. Whatever one does,
whatever one tries to practise, is not aimed at achieving
a higher state or at following some theory or ideal,
but simply, without any object or ambition, trying
to see what is here and now. One has to become aware
of the present moment through such means as
concentrating on the breathing [...] This is based
on developing the knowledge of nowness, for each
respiration is unique, it is an expression of *now*.
Each breath is separate from the next and is fully seen
and fully felt, not in a visualized form, nor simply as
an aid to concentration, but it should be fully and
properly dealt with. Just as a very hungry man,
when he is eating, is not even conscious that he is eating
food. He is so engrossed in the food that he completely
identifies himself with what he is doing and almost
becomes one with the taste and enjoyment of it.
Similarly with the breathing, the whole idea is to try
and see through that very moment in time.

༈

Yearning

*"O David, My Yearning for them is far greater
than theirs can ever be for Me."*

BREATH IS LIFE. HOW MANY TIMES HAVE WE HEARD

this said, how often have we read these words? And yet, their inner meaning so easily passes us by and escapes us in our honest, at times even desperate, yearning to know the truth and to discover the purpose of life on earth.

We meditate, do all sorts of spiritual exercises, read sacred scriptures and sometimes, in our inner and outer suffering, we may even remember to remember the beauty of life. But if we do, do we remember the breath – *at the same time?*

How can we remember life, the life that we all share to-gether, the life that we have been granted for this short time we have on earth, between our first in-breath and our last out-breath, without remembering the breath? Life gives us everything, and yet this is possibly the easiest thing to forget.

Around us it is plain to see just how, over generations and generations, we have almost stripped bare the products and benefits of the life that we have been lent. It shows in the destruction of the ecological etheric web of the planet and in the change of the climate. It reflects in the rapid decrease of space available to us as we fill it up with tech-nological advances like the Internet and endless interpene-trating electronic systems that so many people feel absolutely necessary.

I am not saying they are not necessary. Far from it. What I *am* saying is that there needs to be a correct balance between technology and the yearning for freedom within our hearts. That freedom can only come about through knowledge. And the knowledge I am referring to is the knowledge of oneself. Within the true self, there is unlimited knowledge and unlimited freedom. Once we arrive there, space and time as we know it have no more dominion over us.

Within the heart of the true seeker, there is the breath of freedom that can touch the hearts of every aspect of being. "The worlds are not big enough to contain Me, but the heart of My faithful servant *can* contain Me." Within the heart of the true seeker, there is that eternal remembrance of love as the First Cause. When we remember this on the in-breath, we can breathe out the substance, or the ingredient, which can help bring what is necessary to fan the flame of the Spirit which, for so many, lies dormant, waiting to be born in and through the present moment.

We say, "We search for truth." We say, "We search for God." Words, words, words… We do not have to leave our seat to discover the yearning that is, even at this very moment, permeating the room where we sit. That yearning is universal. That yearning is everywhere and in each moment. And yet, so often, we feel that it is *ours alone.* "O David, My Yearning for them is far greater than theirs can ever be for Me."

Maybe it *was* the search, the pain in the seeking that brought you here, that put this book into your hands. But now, at this time, give up the search and know that it is *you* who is being sought. Let yourself know that you are loved.

How you do this? Simply by letting go, through surrender in its many and varied steps, which in the Sufi tradition are called *fana*. It is the dissolving of the illusion of separation, until the only thing that remains, *baqa,* is the one essential truth that can govern your life on earth and in the worlds-to-come.

Let us remember that we are alive, witnessing God's Life on earth. This makes us His Witnesses. What other creature of His Creation can learn how to remember consciously, to breathe consciously and thus be able to act as real transformers of life on earth? Who else can help restore the balance that is so desperately needed at this time? G.I. Gurdjieff said, "What the plant does unconsciously, we must do consciously." I would add: what is done instinctively in the animal kingdom, we need to understand and act accordingly as true human beings.

༚

I Am In My Breathing

JEANNE DE SALZMANN

I participate in life through breathing. I feel I am in my breathing. It is the way I exist [...] In becoming conscious of the act of breathing, we will understand better the laws governing life and how serving them brings meaning to our existence.

Coming Into Silence

*The most valuable thing is just being,
being in the Presence of God.*

WHAT IS MEDITATION? THERE ARE MANY SORTS OF

meditation. According to what my teacher Bulent Rauf said, it is necessary – family, business, leisure activities or not – that we spend at least a portion of each day, half an hour or so, in meditation. For us, this can mean practising the 7-1-7 breathing. But actually, "coming into silence" is the only expression which is good enough for me. It is, you could say, like a sanctuary.

Beloved Mevlevi Sheikh Suleyman Dede – who was really the closest to a saint I have ever met, a very humble little man, but very tough, too – explained it most simply by saying, "After *dhikr,* just sit!" He would not use the word "meditation", but what he meant was to meditate with the focus on the breath. The most valuable thing after *dhikr* or after prayer is just *being,* being in the Presence of God. We always are, but we need to make our efforts.

The second part of meditation is what I call "reflection". An example of it is when you are sitting quietly in the evening, after the sun has gone down (which is already 'tomorrow' according to the lunar calendar), and you reflect on the day while just breathing. I don't mean to *think* about the day, but to just reflect it and allow all its beauty to pour through and into you.

And so you have these two parts of the same thing which is called "meditation". I know, at times it is so difficult to find the time to do it. There are always excuses we readily find *not* to do it. "O, here's the six-o-clock news coming up" or "I am just so tired today…" But really try and give your best to always find the time, however little it is, to meditate each day and to come into silence.

ॐ

In the House of Breath

ROSE AUSLÄNDER

for Hans Bender

Bridging invisibly
from you to humans and things
from the air to your breath.

Talking with flowers
like with human beings
you love.

Living in the house of breath
one human flower time.

ॐ

The Light Behind the Sun

A Visualization

SIT QUIETLY IN A FAVOURITE PLACE. BE VERY AWAKE
to the present moment. Sense your body and how and
where it is sitting. Look around you, noticing whatever is
there. Remember the senses, and remember the intercon-
nectedness of all life. If you are inside the house, you could
play some beautiful music.

Bring your attention to your breathing. Follow the
breath in and out, like watching the tides on the ocean.
Remember the quality of the breath and that we are all
sharing the same element of air. Breathe in what you
need so that you can breathe out light to the world. Do
not try too hard to make this visualization something
special for yourself alone, but rather make it an exercise in
beauty.

Now bring your attention to the rhythm and placing of
the breath. This puts us in harmony with the universal harmony. Listen to the sound of the *Hu* which is everywhere.

Imagine that you are sitting on a beach by the ocean. It
is that precious time before dawn. The first light is just
creeping up onto the line of the horizon. The air is completely clear and fresh. Breathe in this air deeply. Fill yourself with its purity. Be purified.

There are a few stars still shining. Absorb the light of the
heavens into your being. Feel the earth underneath where
you are sitting. Breathe in the element of the earth. Listen
to the sound of the ocean as you breathe in the element of

water. All these are Gifts of God. He wants us to take them, for this universe is made for us.

As you become more and more aware, sense the light moving over the horizon, getting brighter and brighter as the planet is turning towards the sun. Everything is so still and quiet. Now see the first rays reflected in the ocean. The stars go out one by one. The moon has veiled herself for another day.

Quite suddenly, as the sun cracks the barrier of night and day, it is possible to experience a different quality of sound. So soon the sun rises over the horizon! Feel its warmth on your chest and on your arms and face. Your whole body starts to warm as you sit there on the beach. The first birds are starting to wake. Everything begins to move as the sun gets higher and higher. It is the beginning of a new day.

Very carefully, follow the movement of the sun rising up in front of you, step by step, trying not to lose your attention for the duration of a single breath until it reaches its zenith directly above your head. It is noon. The world is at work.

Slowly, still awake to the rhythm of the breathing, sense the golden rays of the sun permeating every cell of your being. Bring the sun into the centre of your chest and let its rays of living gold pour out into the world. Now you *are* the centre of your own universe! No more are you breathing; you are being breathed. Be very still.

There is a light from a greater sun giving light to your own sun. Open yourself to this light. Let it pour through the crown at the top of your head. This is the "light of pure intelligence", a light without colour as we know it. It is pure, unadulterated light, unfathomable to the normal human imagination, but always there, ready to illuminate us. Through this light we can see the world as a world of patterns, continuously unfolding from the one still moment of creation.

Now we can be *in* the world and yet not *of* the world. We are like a chalice made of the gold of the sun, able to receive the Spirit from the breath of His Compassion.

The exercise is over. Sit quietly for a while in the peace of understanding. Become conscious of your physical body once again. Remember the senses as friends and our responsibility to be custodians of the planet. Look around for a moment and see the world afresh. It is time to get on with our daily lives.

With Visible Breath

Lakota Indians

With visible breath I am walking.
A voice I am sending as I walk.
In a sacred manner I am walking.
With visible tracks I am walking.
In a sacred manner I walk.

Cycles Change

*As cycles develop, so breathing practices will change
to adapt to the given circumstances.*

I HAVE NEVER SAID AND I NEVER WILL SAY THAT I AM
an expert or a professor of *breathing*. There was, for instance, this great German Lady, Professor Ilse Middendorf,
who died in 2009; she certainly was an expert of breathing.
Although I never met her in person, I have met the fruits
of her work, and I have always been very moved in my
heart about who she must have been.

When we look at certain teachings and ask ourselves
about their relevance to the present, we must distinguish
between more or less contemporary people and teachers
who are not living in this present cycle anymore. The
influence of the latter, too, can be profound even today, as
is the case, for example, with Gurdjieff and his pupil
Bennett.

John G. Bennett was a great friend and his school in
England was just three and a half miles away from mine. In
the last few years of his life, Mr. Bennett was trying to give
away everything he knew and had been given. In the age of
seventy-three, he told his friends that he was going to start
a five-year schooling project with one hundred students
staying as residents for ten months in his great house. Most
of the students in the first years' courses were really quite
young. For some reason of his own, Mr. Bennett gave so
many practices, including breathing practices, that you
would need a thick book to remember which one was

which. That was then, in the early 1970s. Would he do the same thing if he was alive today? Very unlikely.

As cycles develop, so breathing practices will change to adapt to the given circumstances. Certain of them remain what I call "relatively standard", certainly in their own country, as for example the various counting methods in Vipassana Buddhism, in Hinduism or in Yoga. The question is: do they travel from one part of the world to another? Some certainly do not, and some, without any doubt, can do more harm than good when being transferred to a different culture. We know perfectly well that a homeopathic remedy made here reverses its polarity on the other side of the equator. In breathing practices in particular, you are dealing with the electromagnetic field and, working through the *chakras* and so forth, you are involving the whole of the system. Most of these practices are very useful, but not all travel. Therefore we need to adapt ourselves to the given circumstances according to where we are and what is happening.

At the time of the flower children, a great 'event' happened. But remember, this is a world of appearances. What you witnessed in those hippie years – that freedom coming out of California, sex and drugs and rock'n'roll, whatever you want to call it – had *already happened* in the higher worlds. Thus, in the late 1960s, something broke through the different interpenetrating worlds in the cosmology of being, and something 'happened' which *seemed* like an event, but which was much more than just an event. At that time, in England and in the United States to a great extent (as well as in most Catholic countries and certainly in the Vatican), meditation was actually considered evil. The local priest near the centre which I ran in

Gloucestershire was eventually thrown out of the Church because he came to my meditation classes! The 'event' that changed everything in the world of appearances, so that it could be recognised by everyone everywhere in the world, had to be 'made' by the higher powers through somebody who everybody in the world knew. And this was the Beatles, one of whom I knew personally.

It was one of the most profoundly important things when the Beatles 'discovered' the Maharishi Mahesh Yogi, who has done a great deal of good for the world no matter what anybody may say. It would have been useless if just anybody had gone off to India – but the Beatles were loved by everyone. When they returned, they brought something from the East, where the sun rises, to the West, and *meditation* became in. Eventually even the Church of England, which lived in square boxes, started to encourage meditation in churches because so few people went to churches anymore anyway. They thought to offer meditations was a way to get people back into their churches. Before that time, very few people in the West had even known the word "meditation" or bothered about "breathing".

In those days, I was asked to give a private breathing class by a Catholic mother superior of a large nunnery in London Notting Hill, which had a very big church. I had been holding public lessons there every Thursday evening and, as is my normal habit, I was in for trouble. The Vatican had just issued an edict that meditation was of the devil and was evil. Do you think that was going to stop me? After she started to attend my public breathing classes, the mother superior's life began to change. Finally one day she said to me, "Reshad, would you please teach my nuns to meditate?" I said, "Yes, but I will only teach them the simple rhythm of the universe, the secret. Strangely enough it is called the 'Mother's Breath'!" Now *that* made her happy, and I continued to explain that it actually came from ancient Egypt. I agreed to come once a week, before the public class, and give a one hour breathing class to all the nuns. She suggested not to do it in the big church, which was huge, but rather in the chapel – which happened to be dedicated to Mary! When I heard that, I felt so humble.

When the nuns arrived in their habits – mother superior was watching me the first time – I said, "Hi nuns!" To begin, I asked them to please pick up their habits and to sit on the laid out cushions. In those days, I was sitting in the half lotus position. So I taught them how to cross their legs the correct way. Finally, they started breathing and, consequently, the whole church started breathing. Although we did not advertise my Thursday evening classes, more and more people came off the streets, the mother superior also joined us and we were all breathing together.

However, there are side-effects to every medication. In those days, I was going through a period in my life when I was simply 'flying', flying on the wings of meditation and breathing – and then I went one step too far. With the many people coming to that church, one day a couple came who wanted me to marry them with a 'new age ceremony'. Everything was "new age" back then, although there is nothing 'new' really. So I said, "Sure, let's marry them in the church!" We were going to have readings and chantings from all the religions, *dhikrs,* candles and whatever... The whole church would be breathing. The mother superior was very happy about this and was getting pretty 'high' herself. But I said, "Mother Superior, there is one request. Can we move the altar?" She said, "Why?"

I replied, "Because I want it to be in the middle, and not at the end of the church. The time of separation is over." We couldn't, obviously, move the very big altar; we would have needed a crane. But we moved another one. And so we had this big ceremony, people joined off the streets, there were flowers everywhere and the couple was married. Hallelujah! *La illaha il' Allah!* Unfortunately, the good mother superior was later summoned to the Vatican and was banished from that nunnery and sent to a very boring and dull monastery in France to pay penance. And that was the end of that cycle.

I am convinced that the secret of understanding the meaning of life is in the moisture on the breath, which is what I have been teaching for forty years. Little by little this is becoming scientific fact because "today's metaphysics is tomorrow's physics". But do you think that in those days, when for many, many years the word "meditation" was on everybody's lips, had I told them what is *inside the breath,* they would have been interested? No! It was a different cycle, and cycles change.

෯

Peace In Ourselves

Hazrat Inayat Khan

It is useless to discuss the peace of the world. What is necessary just now is to create peace in ourselves that we ourselves become examples of love, harmony

and peace. That is the only way of saving ourselves
and the world. Let man try to become more considerate
of others; let him ask himself, "Of what use am I
in the world? Am I born for a certain purpose?", and
then try to train himself to self-control by the mystery
of breath, the best means for accomplishing
that purpose.

࿇

Every Day A Little Bit

Practice makes perfect.

ALL THE BREATHING PRACTICES YOU FIND IN THIS

book are to do with the balance within ourselves. In any
real esoteric school there is a necessity to continue with
practices. It is essential as we go on the spiritual path to
keep this balance. It enables us to be open to the higher
worlds without being swept away in a gale of wind. Man is
a many-dimensional creature, but it is seldom that everything is working in perfect balance. The object of any spiritual practice, therefore, is balance and harmony, enabling
us to live on many planes of consciousness at once.

Also, we should never forget that such practices, basically, are sacred and that all prayer starts with praise. In the
inner tradition, another word for "prayer" is "breath". If
we don't start our day in praising our Creator and remembering Him, perhaps He will forget us! So our attitude in
all these practices should be gratefulness. Even if we feel
miserable, we can start our practices with praise. Maybe

feeling miserable is just the medicine we need to help us get better. If we cannot begin with praise, more than likely we are too serious and thinking only about ourselves and our personal problems.

When doing the practices, you should always try to do your best not to lose your attention for the duration of a single breath. This is difficult because we have so many little I's running around and so little permanent I. But you must not struggle or fight yourself too hard if you are having difficulties. Go on, persevere – every day a little bit. We proceed along life's journey step by step, always doing our best to be awake to the moment, and that is where breathing is so important.

Breathing is a total experience, embracing all aspects of our being. It not only keeps our lungs moving to provide the necessary oxygen for our system, but it also connects us to the worlds outside of us. By focusing our attention on certain parts of the body, we can breathe into and through these areas, activating them and bringing them to life.

One cannot say how long a certain breathing practice, like the ones that are given in this book, should be worked with. Actually, there is no end because there is always something new to learn. Practice makes perfect. I can say, however, that after having practised an exercise repeatedly, you will always be able to come back to the essence of that practice. Once you have assimilated it, which may have taken you a year to learn, the practice becomes real for you. Then you can actually go straight into it and run through it with just one single breath. You will be able, even in very hard times when perhaps you cannot breathe properly because you are in hospital or something very difficult has happened, to bring back the idea or the essence of a practice through creative and conscious memory. It can even start to work on its own, even if *you* cannot. This is possible because the practice has turned into pure memory, and that memory of the practice's harmony is still with you.

I personally always try and remember to do the one or the other of these practices at least a few times a day. However long I have been doing them, I keep coming back to their simple basics, in other words: coming into the rhythm of 7-1-7-1-7, breathing into the solar plexus, in the pause raising my attention to the heart centre and breathing or radiating out light. That's all.

Never forget: we are not doing this to gain power. I pity everybody who does anything for power, because they will land up very miserably. With any practice there is the danger that you can spiritualize the ego rather than transform the heart. That is what Jesus meant when he said so beautifully that you can have all the powers in the world, but without love there is nothing.

Some of you may become very enthusiastic and may want to proceed to other practices, seemingly 'more advanced' ones or practices from other traditions. I am not saying this is wrong – but be aware of ambition! Keep it simple and stick to regularity. That is most important. If you dedicate just a few minutes a day and remember the simplicity of the Mother's Breath, you won't go wrong. You will immediately go into an actively receptive state. If you have the right motive and intention, if you remember to be humble and grateful and if you practice regularly, then undoubtedly you will not only help yourself but also the people around you.

Then the Lord God took some soil from the ground
and formed a man out of it; He breathed life-giving
breath into his nostrils and the man began to live.

GENESIS 2.7

❧

And with that he breathed on them and said, "Receive
the Holy Spirit."

JOHN 20.22

❧

When I have fashioned him in due proportion
and breathed into him of My Spirit, fall ye down
in obeisance unto him.

KORAN 15:29

❧ ❧
❧

Reference

If not stated otherwise below, the discourses presented in this book were compiled and edited from the author's numerous papers and talks over the past forty years. Chapters which were taken, in extracts or in full, from earlier published works by the author and the poems and quotes cited from other authors were taken from the following sources:

17 Reshad Feild: *The Alchemy of the Heart,* Authorhouse, Bloomington, Indiana 2005, chapter "Breath".

22 Muhyiddin Ibn Arabi: *Journey to the Lord of Power,* Inner Traditions International, Rochester, Vermont 1981.

25 Muhyiddin Ibn Arabi: *The Wisdom of the Prophets – Fusus al-Hikam,* Beshara Publications, Gloucestershire 1975.

26 Reshad Feild: *Breathing Alive,* Authorhouse, Bloomington, Indiana 2008, from the addendum "The Mother's Breath".

34 Lorin Roche: *The Radiance Sutras,* www.lorinroche.com

35 Reshad Feild: *Breathing Alive,* Authorhouse, Bloomington, Indiana 2008, chapter "Breathe In – Breathe Out".

40 *The Essene Gospel of Peace,* Book 2, International Biogenic Society 1981.

41 Reshad Feild: *The Inner Work,* Volume I, Chalice Verlag, Zurich 2004, chapter "Standing-Position Breathing Practice".

44 Reshad Feild: *The Inner Work,* Volume II, Chalice Verlag, Freienbach 2010, from the chapter "Living the Breath".

47 Jalaluddin Rumi: *The Mathnawi,* Book I 1951, E.J.W. Gibb Memorial Trust 1990.

47 Reshad Feild: *Reason Is Powerless in the Expression of Love,* Los Angeles 1990, chapter "Breath, The Secret of Life".

52 *The Gift – Poems by Hafiz,* Penguin, New York 1999.

53 Reshad Feild: *Steps to Freedom,* Threshold Books, Putney, Vermont 1983, from the foreword.

54 Shakina Reinhertz: *Women Called to the Path of Rumi,* Home Press, Prescott, Arizona 2001.

59 Reshad Feild: *The Inner Work,* Volume I, Zurich 2004, chapter "Breathing Alive".

68 Frithjof Schuon: *Understanding Islam,* World Wisdom 1994.

69 M.R. Bawa Muhaiyaddeen: *To Die Before Death: The Sufi Way of Life,* The Bawa Muhaiyaddeen Fellowship 1997.

71 Jonathan Star & Shahram Shiva: *A Garden Beyond Paradise. Love Poems of Rumi,* New York 1992.

76 Jalaluddin Rumi: *The Mathnawi,* Book I 865, E.J.W. Gibb Memorial Trust 1990.

77 Reshad Feild: *Steps to Freedom,* Chalice Guild, Decatour, Georgia 1998, chapter "Breath".

82 Nikos Kazantzakis: *The Saviors of God: Spiritual Exercises,* Simon and Schuster, New York 1960, steps 2.30, 3.30, 4.1, 4.2, 4.6–8.

84 *There Is Some Kiss We Want with Our Whole Lives,* Rumi Poems translated and read by Coleman Barks 1999.

87 Kathleen Raine: *Selected Poems,* Lindisfarne Press, Great Barrington, Massachusetts 1988.

95 Ilse Middendorf: *Atem – Stimme der Seele,* Video by Gerd Conradt, 2009. Translation: Robert Cathomas.

96 Reshad Feild: *The Inner Work,* Volume I, Chalice Verlag, Zurich 2004, chapter "Good News – For God's Sake!".

98 Muhyiddin Ibn Arabi: *The Wisdom of the Prophets,* Beshara Publications, Aldsworth, Gloucestershire 1975.

99 Reshad Feild: *The Last Barrier,* Chalice Publishing, Xanten, Germany 2011, page 115 ff.

102 Hazrat Inayat Khan: *Health and Order of Body and Mind,* "The Mystery of Breath".

102 Reshad Feild: *The Inner Work,* Volume I, Chalice Verlag, Zurich 2004, chapter "The 7-1-7 Breathing Practice".

105 Joseph Rael: *Being and Vibration,* Council Oak Books, Tulsa, Oklahoma 1993.

111 Hazrat Inayat Khan: *Health and Order of Body and Mind,* "The Mystery of Breath".

118 Coleman Barks: *The Essential Rumi,* HarperCollins, New York 1997.

119 Reshad Feild: *The Inner Work,* Volume II, Chalice Verlag, Freienbach 2010, chapter "The Reservoir Breathing Practice".

125 Chögyam Trungpa: *Meditation in Action,* Shambhala, Boston & London 1991.

128 Jeanne de Salzmann: *The Reality of Being,* Shambhala, Boston & London 2010.

130 Rose Ausländer: »Im Atemhaus«. From: Rose Ausländer: *Ich höre das Herz des Oleanders. Gedichte 1977–1979.* © S.Fischer Verlag GmbH, Frankfurt am Main 1984. Translation: Robert Cathomas.

131 Reshad Feild: *Breathing Alive,* Authorhouse, Bloomington, Indiana 2008.

138   Hazrat Inayat Khan: *Health and Order of Body and Mind,*
      "The Mystery of Breath".

139   With extracts from: Reshad Feild: *The Inner Work,*
      Volume II, Freienbach 2010, chapter "The Latifa Practice".

Other Books by Reshad Feild

The Last Barrier, 1976
To Know We're Loved – The Invisible Way, 1979
Steps to Freedom, 1983
Here to Heal, 1985
Breathing Alive, 1988
Footsteps in the Sand, 1988
Reason Is Powerless in the Expression of Love, 1990
The Alchemy of the Heart, 1992
Going Home – The Journey of a Travelling Man, 1996
The Inner Work – Study Material of a Living Esoteric School, 2004

Contact

Contact details of study groups working under the guidance of
Reshad Feild can be found at **www.chalice.ch** (for Europe) and
www.chalice.net (for the United States).

www.chalice-publishing.com